Rincon Point

Rincon Point

Shaun L. Swegman

Copyright © 2021 Shaun L. Swegman

All Rights Reserved

ISBN: 978-0-578-94997-0

Cover art and book design by Shaun L. Swegman

For the sailing crew.

1

Broken

The Southern California sunlight streaming through the hospital window did little to cheer up the setting. In the bed, under a blanket, bandages, and various tubes and IVs, lied a young man, 19 years old, in a medically induced coma. The only part of him really visible was his face, a handsome face in life, but now slack, unconscious, sandy blond hair poking up around his head in the places the bandages didn't cover.

Next to the bed, a coarse-looking, well-dressed man sat in a chair, quietly reading a *Spin* magazine to the young man in a coma. The well-dressed man raised his head to the sound of the door opening, another young man walking in.

"Oh, I'm sorry," the young man said. "I didn't know he had company."

"No, come in," said the well-dressed man. "He needs all the support he can get."

The young man nodded somberly. He too was handsome, noted the well-dressed man. "Do you know who I am?" asked the well-dressed man.

"H-his father?" the young man said, in the tone of a question, but not really a question.

"I am," the well-dressed man said. "You can call me Vin."

"Nice to meet you, Mr., uh, Vin," said the young man, reaching out for a handshake that was perfunctorily returned. "I'm Dave Sims. Your son and I are close friends."

The young man was either too smart or too scared to ask something stupid, like *How is he doing?* The answer to that was clear. He was in a fucking hospital bed with tubes stuck in him. He was not doing well.

"I'm going to get these fuckers," said the well-dressed man.

Vin Capriani was used to being the scariest man in the room. He was not used to being surprised, or scared himself. But what happened next gave him a chill. The young man who came to visit his son, whom Capriani had written off as another pretty-boy surfer flake, and possibly even a *finocch,* took on a look he'd seen before. A look worn only by very dangerous men, in Capriani's experience. And in a voice that oozed frost and menace, the young man replied:

"Not if I get them first. There won't be anything left if I do."

The young man who called himself Sims looked at his friend in the hospital bed again, then turned around and left just as abruptly as he'd arrived.

2

Leaving Home

It should have been one of the better days in Terry Cahill's life. It ended up being one of the worst. His big breakthrough story on local corruption had been published in the *Ventura County Monitor* only the week before, and already subpoenas were rolling out to some of the miscreants involved.

Unfortunately for Terry, some of those now facing court had connections to his paper's publisher, who, sadly, was not a beacon of ethics himself. And so it happened that just days after printing his story, which was rolling up crooked businessmen along with a couple of city councilors into the arms of the justice system, the *Monitor* fired Terry on the publisher's orders. His editor, Irwin Martin ("Call me Marty"), had not seemed particularly put out at giving Terry the news.

Feeling pretty thoroughly defeated, he went home that morning, now jobless. As he pulled up in front of the house he shared with his wife on McKinley Drive at the corner of Virginia, he was only mildly surprised to find a black Porsche convertible in his driveway.

Des must be here for a visit, he thought. After all, it looked like his father-in-law's car.

So it was quite a shock when Terry walked into his home to find his wife playing house with Chase Conners, a friend whom she'd supposedly known since childhood.

"Terry ..." said Mallory Cahill, who'd been caught by surprise herself, wrapping her body up in a bedsheet. She couldn't think of anything to say at the moment. That was OK, the moment spoke for itself.

His world had pretty much stopped then. It was more bad news than he was willing to process in one morning. It was one thing to lose a job. Terry felt himself losing his whole life in the span of hours. At some point he noticed Mal talking again, but he couldn't really make out any of the words. His head was humming away as his own thoughts took over, drowning out everything else. He was also vaguely aware of Conners sputtering and trying to fumble back into his clothes.

Terry simply held up a hand, as if to say, "Not now," and turned for their bedroom closet. It was as if his brain short-circuited and defaulted to autopilot. He scooped up as many of his clothes as would fit in his battered old Samsonite, and stuffed them in as Mallory followed him around trying to talk about what had just transpired. She might as well have been talking to herself, as Terry was still completely tuned out. He stopped by the bathroom for his toothbrush. *I'll definitely need this,* he thought, putting the toothbrush and his deodorant in the case. *What else?* His eyes caught a glint from the polished finish of his guitar. *That.*

He grabbed the suitcase and picked up the guitar on his way toward the kitchen telephone. He'd need a cab.

As he was reaching for the phone, Mallory tried again. Now clothed in a robe, she came into the kitchen.

"Please, don't," she said. "Don't leave. Let's talk. We can work things out. I know it looks bad ..."

Terry picked up the phone and dialed for a taxi. When the dispatcher answered, he gave her the address of a nearby convenience store and said, "Yes. As soon as possible, please. Thank you." He hung up.

Mallory tried again. "Please don't go," she whispered.

"Goodbye, Mal," he said. "Have a great life."

He walked out the door. As he was going down the driveway, he hawked up a loogie and spat it on the driver's seat of the Porsche.

3

Sighting

There were no lifeguards on-duty early in the morning on Rincon Point Beach, no one to point out the approaching fins. Not that it mattered. The sharks' approach was too deep for that cliché anyway. The only people watching the water were looking for the next wave, nothing else. And most of that small group was already bobbing in the water on their surfboards.

The first bite took one of the surfers' legs off below the knee with bone-crunching rip. His scream was cut short above water by his surfboard capsizing and him being dunked in the drink, but he continued to scream underwater, which may have saved his life for the time being. The shark, no longer sure about his meal, swam in another direction. But it wasn't the only shark there, and as the surfers frantically tried to paddle their way to shore they made themselves look more like prey, and there were more bites.

In all, three of the surfers were injured by shark bites, and another four had more or less minor injuries from mishaps such as colliding into each other or slipping and falling down in their haste to escape, even once on land.

Jon-Jon, the one missing half his leg, was in the worst shape, and the other surfers knew that if somebody didn't get help quickly he'd probably die on the beach.

The man watching through binoculars from a car parked across the highway hoped he would. His car was sitting a few yards down from a CHP call box that had been disabled. Somebody had used a set of bolt cutters to sever the cord between the box and handset. It was the only phone nearby.

4

Now What

Terry walked to the parking lot of the local Circle K on Main and Seaward just as his cab was pulling in. At least, he hoped it was his cab. It wouldn't surprise him if Mal had gotten dressed, hopped in the car and was on her way to try to intercept him, and he just wasn't able to handle a confrontation at the moment. All he wanted was a clean getaway.

And luck, for once on this most rotten day, was on his side. It was his cab. He tossed the suitcase on the back seat and climbed in after it holding his guitar.

"Where to?" the cabbie asked.

Terry gave him the name of a cheap, somewhat disreputable motel on the waterfront. On his walk to the convenience store, he had checked his wallet to see what his resources were. Inside was $87 in cash, and one uncashed paycheck from the week before. The sum total was not impressive, and without a job he knew he needed to make whatever he had last as long as possible. Due to the delay between pay periods ending and checks going out, he knew he'd have one more paycheck coming. After that, that would be it. The credit cards in his wallet were billed to a joint account with his wife. He'd be cutting those up. He had only himself to rely on.

There was one other benefit to the motel, besides being cheap. It was near the Ventura marina, and he knew a friendly bar in the area. After the day he'd had, he definitely needed a drink. As the cab pulled away from the curb, Terry noticed the song playing on the oldies station. It was The Byrds "I'll Feel A Whole Lot Better." Terry laughed. It was just a little too on the nose.

The cab took Seaward across the 101, then hooked a left on Harbor Boulevard toward the Ventura Marina and the Docksider Motel, an early-'50s building with peeling turquoise paint on its wooden-slat sidings. It was just after lunchtime when Terry had finally checked in, tossed his suitcase on the folding rack, and collapsed into the bed. He wasn't hungry. A nap sounded just fine.

When he opened his eyes again, it was early evening. He didn't feel refreshed, exactly, and the few winks hadn't given him any clarity or perspective on the shit burrito his day, and his life, had become. But he was slightly less tired, and that's about the best he could've expected. He knew it.

He didn't really need a shower, but he took one anyway. It seemed to be the thing to do after waking up, and he didn't really know what his next move was yet. In the back of his mind, he knew he should probably eat something, since he hadn't eaten anything that day and drinking was on the agenda. But he still didn't feel hungry.

Maybe just a burger, he thought. His stomach lurched in response. *OK, maybe not.*

Things weren't exactly jumping at the Beam Reach, but it was reasonably full for a weeknight. The bar at the Ventura marina was built to look like an oversized shanty, with dried out old wood, huge ropes, and strings of white lights being the chief features of the second-floor deck. The inside was more like a Tiki bar. It had been built this way in the early '60s and the theme and decor never changed, which gave it an atmosphere that was both authentic and slightly seedy.

The bar had been bought two years ago by a young woman named Wendy MacNamara, who also ran charters on her sailboat, a 41-foot ketch named *Clara* which also functioned as her home, from the harbor. She had rescued the bar from the brink of bankruptcy when she purchased it. It had occurred to Terry that Wendy was the kind of person who must've had a great story. You could tell just from the way she talked, moved, did things, that she had seen a lot. But Terry's beat had been cops and courts, not human interest stories, so while his curiosity was professionally inspired, he really had no reason to pursue it.

Terry was able to get a seat a the bar, and was only mildly surprised to find himself sitting next to his friend, the sheriff of Ventura County.

"Evening, Terry," said Sheriff Tim Baker, raising a bottle of Dos Equis with a lime floating in the neck. "How's it hanging?"

Tim Baker did not look like a sheriff. He looked more like someone you'd find playing Beach Boys covers on an acoustic guitar at a seaside bar. His skin was deeply tanned and his hair bleached from the sun. When he wasn't in uniform, he favored cargo shorts, loud Aloha shirts, and boat shoes. He was of average height and build, and his eyes spoke of a certain playfulness that led many to be surprised to learn he was a cop. A damn good cop, at that.

Terry Cahill had met Sheriff Baker during the course of his work on the cops and courts beat. Cops and reporters don't always have the coziest of relationships, but Cahill had earned Baker's respect by being scrupulously fair in his reporting. If a cop fucked up, Cahill would document it. However, he was just as sure to mention when they were doing the right thing. Baker, never one for suck-ups or phonies, appreciated the candor. Cahill's only agenda seemed to be to tell the truth, and Baker himself would flay a deputy for betraying his oath of service. He knew that good cops should be the last people on Earth to tolerate bad cops.

The two formed an unlikely friendship over post-case beers, usually at the Reach. It was how Terry himself had found out about the place. The sheriff was an avid sailor, and Wendy sometimes crewed for Baker on his sloop, *Easy Goer.*

"My life," he replied, "Has become a country and western song."

"Can't be that bad," Tim said.

At that moment, Wendy appeared behind the bar across from Terry. "Hiya, sailor," she winked. "What'll it be?"

"You still make those nasty-strong Jet Pilots?" he asked. She nodded in the affirmative.

"I'll start with a double."

"We don't make doubles of those, hon," Wendy said. "They're already triples."

"OK, maybe it is that bad," Tim said. "Whatcha got?"

Terry told his friend about his day, starting with getting fired and ending with him checking into a motel after leaving his wife. When he was finished, Baker said, "At least you didn't lose your dog, too."

"We didn't have a dog," Terry said.

"Let's get you another one of those Jet Pilots." The sheriff signaled to Wendy for a refresher. "So, why not go work for the *Times?* You're a good reporter. I'm sure you could do better there than you ever did here."

"I've already been in the Army once. It wasn't for me. I don't want to become a part of another strictly hierarchal organization like that, and from what I've heard, the *Times* is worse than the Army."

"Thanks a lot," Tim said.

"Huh?"

"Well, my other suggestion was going to be you join us as a deputy. I mean, you already have law-enforcement experience as an MP."

Terry recognized the taste of shoe leather, and felt bad he'd offended his friend.

"That actually sounds like a better job to me, but I'm not sure I'm the right fit."

"Yeah, I get it. Lone-wolf Cahill wants to go it alone. You find authority stifling."

"Something like that."

"So how long do you plan to stay in that motel?"

"I don't really know. I don't have much money, maybe enough to get me through the next two or three weeks at the motel's rates. After that? I need to find a new job, like, right away." He took a deep sip of his Jet Pilot.

"Uh, don't close the door on that deputy offer right away."

"This is a crazy idea," the sheriff started. "But why don't you save your money and stay on my boat until you get on your feet again."

Terry was taken aback by the offer. "You sure about that?" he asked.

"Wouldn't offer if I wasn't," Tim said. "

"Thanks. I'll think it over."

"Think it over, bullshit," Baker said. He reached in his pocket and pulled out a keyring. Attached were keys to get onto the dock at the marina, as well as keys to *Easy Goer*. "Go ahead and move in tomorrow. Not like you'll be doing much else, anyway. It'll give you some breathing room while you figure things out."

"Thank you, Tim," Terry said. "I'll figure them out quickly. But thank you for the help."

"Terry, it's what friends are for," said the sheriff.

5

A New Morning

Terry woke up alone in his dingy motel room, his mouth dried out from the overly conditioned air, which smelled only faintly of decades of stale cigarette smoke. His head felt like somebody had been setting off Cherry Bombs in his skull as he slept. Not normally a big drinker, the previous night's activities were extracting a price. The pillow had to be peeled from his face as he sat up in the bed and groaned.

He was, at first, disoriented. But within a few seconds of waking up he remembered everything. Why he was here, and why his head hurt. He had fallen asleep with his clothes still on. Something stiff was in his left hip pocket, and it was poking at him. He reached in and pulled out a small plastic envelope with two aspirin in it. Wendy had given it to him last night before he left the bar.

Thank you, he thought.

Shit. I need a job.

He downed the aspirin with a couple handfuls of tap water and looked at himself in the mirror. He was 28 years old, just over six feet tall, thin and lanky. His dark blond hair had gotten longer than he usually kept it. He thought about shaving off the mustache he'd had since his days in the Army. It was unfashionable now. He had a handsome face, not like a movie star, but a face that conveyed a sort of gentle kindness. It had been an asset as a reporter, as he found people, particularly women, were more likely to open up and talk to him than some of his colleagues at the newspaper. Now his eyes were slightly red, and his face lined with worry.

He went outside looking for a vending machine that sold the *Times*. He needed the classifieds to start his job search, as well as his search for a new car and his search for a new place to live. But he would be damned if he spent even one penny on the paper that had fired him. Those fuckers could starve, for all he cared. *When I get another job, I might even subscribe to their competitor from the big city,* he thought.

Terry was contemplating a shower and its possible rejuvenating effects when the phone rang in his room. It was not a welcome sound.

Has to be a wrong number, he thought. *Maybe the front desk? Sheriff Tim?* He picked up the phone. It was Desmond Getz.

"Well, this is a bit of a surprise," Terry said to his father-in-law.

"I'm disappointed you didn't expect my call," Desmond said. "After what happened, it's only natural for me to want to get in touch."

"Yeah, that's not the surprising part," Terry said. "I'm just surprised you knew where to find me."

"The cheapest motel in town?" Desmond asked. "Not a real stretch. You were at the first place I tried."

"OK, I should have known my own predictability there. So, obviously I can infer the reason for your call, but I still don't know what to say. What is it you'd like to tell me?"

"I wanted to ask you if it's really over."

"Yes," Terry said. "Absolutely."

"No chance you might reconsider? I mean, you are married. You know, till death and all that?"

"Des, there is no chance I will get back together with her. I'll never trust her again. You know what happened, don't you? I can't imagine how she'd spin the story."

"I have a pretty good idea. I know who my daughter is. She didn't spell it out for me, but I gather you found her in the arms of another."

"That's an admirably diplomatic way of putting it," Terry said. "Yes, that pretty much sums it up right there."

"Infidelity doesn't have to be a dealbreaker, Terry," Des said. "Not if you love her."

"It is a dealbreaker for me. The biggest one." He thought for a moment. "Maybe I don't love her. In fact, I can't imagine myself loving her now. Not after what she did."

"So, you hate her?" Desmond asked, sadness in his voice.

"No. All I want is to forget her. Hate won't let you do that, it doesn't let you move forward." Terry paused again. "I want to move forward so fast that this whole part of my life is behind me as soon as humanly possible."

"And then?"

"And then, I want to never look back at it."

"And you're sure of this?"

Terry laughed. "I've never been sure about anything in my life. But I'm sure about this. Mal and I are over, forever. I'll be filing divorce papers before the week is over."

Des made an uneasy sound over the line.

"By the way, I'm glad you called," Terry said. "Can you recommend me a very good lawyer?"

"Terry, she's still my daughter."

"Not for the divorce," Terry said. "I won't need a good lawyer for that. I don't want anything. Not the house, not the cars, not the money. She keeps it all. I already took my clothes and my guitar, anyway. All I want is a clean break and my name back."

"That seems a bit extreme," Des said. "You're entitled to half of the couple's combined assets."

"No, I'm not," Terry said. "It's not my money and it never was. It's yours, and I'm not going to rip you off just because things didn't work out between your daughter and me. I'm not going to rip her off just because I caught her, uh, 'in the arms of another.' I want this over as quickly as possible. I figure none of that stuff was ever mine anyway, and letting her have everything should be a pretty decent way to keep this thing from dragging on."

"I can always buy her another house," Des said.

"And maybe someday, you will. But not on account of yours truly."

"You really don't want anything from her?"

"I'd like it if she'd change her name back."

"I don't think you can actually make her do that."

"I probably can't, but maybe she'll take some mercy on me, seeing as how she gets to keep everything, and grant me that one request."

"She doesn't have everything, Terry. She doesn't have you. She's pretty miserable right now."

"And that's the result of her own actions."

"I never said otherwise. But you really can't forgive her?"

"Forgive?" Terry said. "Maybe someday. Like I said, I don't want to carry this around with me. But forgiving her doesn't mean we get back together. It only means I might take her phone call someday down the line."

"So what do you need a good lawyer for?"

"Oh, that," Terry said. "I'm going to sue the shit out of my former employer for wrongful termination."

"Termination? You were fired?"

"Same day I left Mal. That's why I was home early. Probably why I caught her."

"Why were you fired?" Des asked.

"My last story on corrupt councilors taking bribes rolled up some of the publisher's business associates. He didn't like that. Marty said I was being let go for 'general insubordination,' but that's bullshit. They always gave me some hell, thought I wasn't 'tough' enough on the cops, but I have no record of write-ups or any disciplinary action."

"Well, that's certainly unfair. Maybe even unethical. But it's not grounds for a suit. You'd need to be fired for something directly related to being a member of a protected class for a judge to even hear the case."

"OK, get this," Terry said. "My editor told me more than once that he 'knew he couldn't trust a veteran' to cover the cops. That all us guys in uniform were all the same."

Desmond smiled on the other end of the line. "That, my friend, might be worth pursuing. It's weak, don't get me wrong. In fact, if it went to trial, we'd probably lose. But I get the idea that your publisher isn't a man of particularly strong ethics, am I correct?"

"He's about as trustworthy as a salesman's smile, and I think he's probably connected to some of the shady dealings my last big story uncovered, so I'd say you're on the right track with that assumption."

"Well, if he's as crooked as you believe, a suit filed by an attorney with an appropriately intimidating reputation might just frighten him into a settlement out of court. Even if he knows we'd lose, there's all kinds of things that can come out in a courtroom. Especially if you're facing a sharp lawyer on the other side."

"Great. You have someone in mind?"

"Yes," Des replied. "Me."

"You're certainly good enough, but I'm not sure I can afford your rates, Des."

"For you, I'll do this for free."

"I can't accept that. I don't want to take advantage."

Terry heard a note of sadness enter his father-in-law's voice.

"Terry, you said you never want to think of the life you had with my daughter again. I accept that, but don't you understand? This could be the last chance I have to spend any time with you before you go off and forget us all. I'm going to miss you. So let me do this, OK?"

Terry felt like a heel hearing that.

"Shit, Desmond, I'm sorry. I don't know what I'm saying. I want to forget about the bad stuff, but I don't want to forget you and Sharon. You feel more like family to me than my actual family."

"All the same, we probably won't see each other very much once the divorce is final. That's just the way those things go."

"Yeah, it is."

"So let me do this, Terry. No charge. It gives me an excuse to see you before we go our separate ways."

"OK, sure."

The conversation with his soon-to-be ex-father-in-law left Terry drained. He had just woken up, but thinking about his situation with Mallory was exhausting. The fact that he liked Desmond didn't exactly help.

• • •

Terry, the youngest of four children, had come along late in his parents' lives, and he had lost them both while he was overseas in the Army. He wasn't close to his siblings, the youngest of whom was 15 years older than him. His parents were pretty much checked-out of the whole parenting thing by the time he'd come along, and he had grown up almost as an only child. Des and his wife Sharon had taken to him immediately when he and Mallory started seeing each other, and Terry grew close to both of them very quickly. Sometimes he wondered how much of his motivation for marrying Mal had been to replace the sense of family he'd never really felt in his own.

He sat on the bed and picked up the issue of the *Times* he had just bought. The inside Metro section slid out of the bundle, and a headline on the first page caught his eye.

Sharks Attack At Rincon

He read the story, about 10 inches on three surfers who were bitten by what appeared to be juvenile great whites. *This is probably the* Monitor's *PI, above the fold,* he thought. One surfer had lost a leg to the attack, but was expected to survive, in stable condition at St. Francis Medical Center in Santa Barbara. He browsed a few more stories throughout the sections of the paper, then pulled out the classified ads to save and tossed the rest in a wastebasket. He decided it was time for that shower.

Terry had some errands to run after checking out of the motel room. He walked over to the marina to drop off his suitcase and guitar aboard *Easy Goer*, using the keys Sheriff Baker had given him the night before.

The boat was a Beneteau 350, a 35-foot sloop with a furling mainsail, a small, easy-handling yacht with sleek lines that reminded Terry of a racer. Sheriff Baker had purchased it new three years ago, and it was his most prized possession. Sheriff Baker's wife, Cindy, did not share his love of sailing due to her incurable seasickness.

In an attempt to redirect his interests to more land-based hobbies, Cindy had taken her husband to the horseraces. Tim hadn't been terribly interested in the horses, and his position in law enforcement had brought him into contact with more than a few lives that had been damaged by a gambling addiction.

So in an effort to dissuade his wife, he bet the entire $500 he'd brought with him on a 30-1 shot in a single race. But the horse, a young stallion named Easy Goer that would later become moderately famous, had won. Tim took his winnings and used them as a down payment on the boat, which he named after the horse that had paid for it. After that his wife accepted that maybe having different interests wasn't the worst thing.

It wasn't his first time aboard *Easy Goer*. Terry had been sailing a few times with the sheriff. Wendy had been a part of that crew too. He looked around at his new temporary digs below decks. There were fore and aft cabins, a tiny galley, a living area, and a head. The boat was clean and tidy, everything in its place. He couldn't imagine living there for very long, but for the time being it would do.

Once his gear was stowed, Terry climbed out and locked everything back up. He walked over to the Beam Reach to use the payphone outside and called for a cab. When it arrived, he asked to be taken to the nearest bank, but the closest one was a branch of the same bank he had used with his soon-to-be ex-wife, and he didn't want there to be any mixups. So he asked to be taken to the next nearest bank, where he used the uncashed paycheck in his wallet to open a new account.

Knowing he would need to buy a car, he decided to draw half of the check in cash, leaving the rest in his new checking account. Once he was all set up there, he left, deciding to walk back to the marina instead of paying for another cab. Along the way he passed a drugstore, and realized he'd need to pick up some basics beyond toothpaste and deodorant if he were no longer going to be staying in a motel. He bought a pack of disposable razors, a small can of shaving cream, a bottle of Aqua Velva, a travel-sized bottle of shampoo, a bar of soap, a shower tote bag, and a cheap pair of foam rubber flip flops.

Not feeling like doing anything else, he headed back to the Beam Reach, thinking maybe he'd have a burger there for an early dinner. He hadn't eaten anything for nearly two days, and suddenly he realized that he was famished.

While he was at the bar, his pager went off. He checked the number. It was Mallory. He decided to call her back.

Can't just avoid her forever, I guess, he thought.

6

For the Record

Terry called his former home from the payphone outside the Beam Reach. His wife answered on the first ring.

"Hi, Terry," she said.

"How did you know it was me?" Terry asked.

"Blind faith," she said, a question in her voice. "I just paged you. I hoped it was you calling. I didn't know."

"What do you need, Mallory?"

"*We* need to talk about what happened, Terry."

"I don't feel any particular need to discuss it. It's not like anything we could say will change what happened. What is there even to talk about?"

"I was hoping you just needed a little time, and then maybe we could work things through. But I talked to dad today ..." she trailed off. "He said you never want to see me again. Is that really true, Terry?"

"I said something to that basic effect when he called, yeah."

"But is it *true?* Is that how you really feel? Never again? Just done? You're just going to throw me away? You want to throw our whole life together away like a ... like, something you don't need anymore?"

Terry sighed.

"All I know at this point is that the trust between you and I is broken, and it'll never be whole again. And I cannot be with someone I don't trust completely. We cannot be together again. Even if I tried, I ... I just wouldn't be there."

"Weren't you ever happy being with me?" she asked. Terry thought about it a moment.

"Yeah, of course I was. We had some really good years, some really good times. Until the other day, I didn't know anything was wrong with us. I'd say most of the time I was with you, I was happy. I should be asking you that. I mean, I'm not the one who went looking for something outside our marriage."

"But you're not asking it," she said.

"I guess I already know the answer, and the answer doesn't really matter anyway. It's all just words now. They don't change anything. What is, simply is."

"But I wasn't unhappy with you, Terry. I'm unhappy without you."

"I guess you need to ask yourself why you felt that I wasn't enough for you, then," Terry said softly.

"I have an addiction ... to, oh this is hard to say." She paused, and Terry let the silence stand until she picked back up again. "I have a sexual addiction, and I act out because of it. I've been doing it my, well, almost my whole life."

"That sounds like an issue you might try exploring with a therapist, Mal. I'm not your therapist. I'm just your soon-to-be ex-husband."

"You don't even care," she said, this time accusingly.

"Depends on what you mean. I care that someone I used to love is hurting, sure. That's why I suggested a therapist. But I don't care why you cheated on me. The reason for that doesn't interest me."

"Listen to you. 'Used to love.' I don't see how you can just turn off something like that. I still love you."

"I imagine you'll get over that soon enough." As soon as he said it, he regretted it.

"That was low, Terry." she said almost inaudibly.

"I ... shit, I'm sorry, Mal. That was ... I'm sorry."

"I remember you talking about the drug cases you wrote about for the paper. You said those people were addicts, they were sick. You said it wasn't fair to treat sick people like criminals, that they were exactly the kind of people who needed the support of the community most. You said it always made you really sad to see those people lose the support of loved ones, because it just guaranteed they'd get worse.

"Well, Terry, I'm sick. I need the support of people who love me. How is my addiction any different from theirs?"

Terry didn't have an answer for that that he felt very good about.

"Well, Terry?"

"I can't have a relationship without trust, Mallory. I just can't. I can't be with you anymore. But I will support you in other ways, if you really want help. I'll do what I can. But I can't be with you. I can't stay married to you. What we had is gone forever. Whatever we have in the future, if there is a future, will be something else."

"You said we had some good years together, right?" she asked. "Well, I was acting out pretty much the whole time. Chase Connors was my first lover. We've been together since before you met me. There were others, but it was mostly him. He was the reason I went to school in Texas. I followed him there. In a way, if it weren't for him, we never would have met."

"That doesn't exactly make me want to leap back into your arms, Mal. Why are you even telling me that?"

"If you could be happy with me not knowing that, why can't you be happy with me knowing it? Why can't you be happy and just pretend not to know it?"

"That's not how relationships work for most people," he said. "I can't be happy sharing my partner. That's not me. Look, it's becoming pretty obvious that I was never the right guy for you. If that's the kind of relationship you want, you should be looking for someone who feels the way you do."

"Just think about it, please."

"There's nothing to think about. I'm not changing my mind. Goodbye, Mallory."

"Wait, Terry. Where are you staying? How are you doing? Are ... are you OK?"

"I'm OK, thanks. You could say that a friend took me in. I feel pretty crappy, I guess. I'm still hurting, dealing with it the best I can. But you don't need to worry about me, OK. I'll be all right."

"I'll never not worry about you. Take care of yourself, Terry. I'm not there to take care of you."

"I'll be OK. But ... thanks for thinking of me." He hung up the line before anything else could be said.

The phone call left him emotionally wrung out. Twice in one day now. He hoped there wouldn't be any more calls for a while. The fact that she had been cheating on him the entire time they were together was an unwelcome bombshell. He found himself thinking about all the time they had been together, and felt the whole thing was just one massive betrayal.

•••

Terry Cahill met Mallory Getz while they were both students at The University of Texas. Terry had chosen the school because Texas had been his last state of residence before going overseas to Germany with the Army. He had been stationed at Ft. Hood in Killeen prior to shipping out, and he had liked the Hill Country. And Texas was offering in-state tuition. So when he was discharged and sent back to the states, he applied and was accepted at the University in nearby Austin.

Mallory Getz was captivating. She was the center of attention just about everywhere she went, an olive-skinned beauty with dark hair and green eyes that seemed to change color with her mood or the weather. Terry met her while working at a bar in West Campus. He fell hard for her, as men were prone to doing. Looking back, he was always kind of surprised that she said 'yes' when he asked her out. They started dating, became an item, and spent their last two years of college together.

When they graduated, Mallory intended to move back home to Montecito. Terry had no real plan or direction other than trying to get a job in journalism. Though his family had moved all over the country when he was growing up, he had never been to California. Mallory invited him to come with her. Terry proposed.

They got married barely six months after graduation. Terry had liked the Getz family as soon as he met them, and liked his new life with Mallory. He found the job writing for the cops 'n courts beat for the *Ventura County Monitor* shortly after their move to California. Mallory's parents had bought them the house on McKinley as a wedding present. For a while there, it had seemed as if everything was just working itself out.

But Terry knew now that things were never that easy. He had grown complacent. He had taken his life for granted, and all the good things in it. At some point, he had stopped putting in the effort. And now he saw that he had no family left, and few friends. It may be true that no man is an island, but Terry was more isolated than most.

7

Talking Cars

"So, why didn't you keep the truck?" Tim asked.

Terry and Tim were having a beer at the Beam Reach, watching the sun slowly drop to the horizon over the harbor. It was a warm evening, maybe a little warmer than one would expect sitting just off the water. That made the beer taste even better.

"The short version is, she bought it for me, and I don't want anything at all that reminds me of her," Terry said.

"You know, for a journalist, you sure are a fan of the fucking short version," Tim said. "Aren't you supposed to be a storyteller?"

Terry shrugged. "I ever tell you about the time she bought me a Porsche?"

Tim nearly choked on his beer.

"No, I don't believe I heard that one," Tim said. "Do tell."

"This one time, she bought me a fucking Porsche. The end."

"I think there might be more to this story..."

"There is," Terry said. He took a long pull on his beer, staring off at the reflection of the sun in the Pacific Ocean.

"When I got out of the Army, summer of '84, I bought myself two things: a used Gibson J200 guitar, which I didn't need, can barely play, and still thankfully have; and a brand-new 1985 4Runner, which I regrettably do not still have. I loved that 4Runner. First and only car I ever bought new. She hated it, of course."

"I thought women loved those rugged, outdoorsy types," Tim said with a smirk.

"Not her. It was kinda noisy, not super comfortable, it was slow, the A/C wasn't great, and by the time we were married the paint had faded pretty badly. You remember that red paint Toyota used to use?"

Tim grunted.

"But I loved it. It was mine, had never been anybody else's, and I planned to drive that thing into the ground. I was going to keep it at least 20 years. Didn't ever want to sell it, just drive it until it can't drive anymore.

"So it was six months after we were married," Terry continued. "Our six-month anniversary, she called it. She said she wanted to spoil me."

"Buying you an expensive sports car should be a good move in that direction," Tim said.

"Not really. I mean, maybe for some guys, but not me. Like I said, I liked my 4Runner. It was like a perfectly broken-in pair of jeans, y'know. Anyway, I come home from work that night, flowers, chocolates, bottle of some decent Champagne."

Tim snorted.

"I swear," Terry said. "It was even French. So I get home from work, thinking I'm doing all right on the being thoughtful stuff. You know. It wasn't like Valentine's Day, or a real anniversary, but I knew she was sentimental about that kind of thing and thought I was doing well to bring home, I dunno, the traditional things."

"Traditional, once you're married, means jewelry," Tim said.

"Yeah, sure, for like, a real anniversary. Not six months. Six fucking months?" Terry finished off his beer and nodded toward the bartender for another Schlitz.

"Continue, please," Tim prompted, taking a sip of his own beer.

"So, I get home, I'm in a good mood, I'm thinking things are going to be fine tonight. And then I see a fucking Porsche in the driveway. And I'm like, 'Oh, I guess we have company. Great. There go all my plans for the night.' I was a little pissed, really. So I go inside, and it's just her there. No company.

"She sees me come in, runs over to greet me, and says, 'Did you see the car?' 'Yeah, I saw the car,' I said. 'Whose is it?' And she says, 'Yours! Happy anniversary.' And I'm just like, ah, shit."

"You don't want the sports car," Tim says, shaking his head. "Only you."

"I had to explain to her," Terry said. "I had just gotten my job at the paper, I was still a green reporter working cops 'n courts. If I showed up to court or the station in that penis-stretcher ..."

"Everybody you had to work with would think you're an asshole," Tim finished for him.

"A gigantic, gaping asshole," Terry agreed.

Both paused for more sips of beer.

"So I told her, you know, look, it's really thoughtful. I really, deeply appreciate where this came from. But I can't accept it. I can't be that kind of guy, I can't drive that kind of car. It just does not work with my job.

"And of course she finds this all upsetting. It doesn't turn into a full-blown fight, but the heaviness of hurt feelings was inescapable. I felt incredibly shitty."

"And yet, you could not go any other way," Tim said.

"No, I really couldn't," Terry said. More beer. A thoughtful pause. "OK, maybe I could've."

"How do you figure?"

"I could have gone to work for her father's firm, driven a Porsche, worn fancy clothes. I could have tried to fit into her world, instead of expecting her to fit into mine, or us to somehow work together staying in our different worlds. I could have been Porsche guy. It just would have meant changing almost everything about myself."

"And you think maybe you should have?"

"Hell no. I would've been miserable."

"Atta boy," Tim said, signaling the bartender for his own refresh.

"Anyway, she ends up giving the car to Desmond, which is a fairly unfunny joke," Terry said. "She bought the damn thing with his money, and if he wanted one, he'd probably already have one. But Desmond loves his daughter, and dutifully accepted the regifted Porsche. He'd drive it when he came to visit us, probably so she wouldn't ask why he never drove it. I doubt he ever drove it anywhere else."

"He still got it?" Tim asked.

"Probably. You in the market?"

"You know me," Tim said. "I spend my money on boats, not cars."

"Well, you spend your money on *a* boat."

"Like throwing money into a hole in the ocean, they say." Tim drank more beer. "Well, you're not a bad storyteller after all."

"Story's not over yet," Terry said before taking a swig. Tim raised an eyebrow. "Anyway, she gives the Porsche to daddy, but she doesn't exactly give up. So about a week later, I've got to go to Sac on assignment, cover part of a story happening in the lege. I'm gone four days, and since the paper was paying for the trip, I flew. Let Mal drop me off at the airport so I wouldn't have to pay for parking. Second biggest mistake of my life, turns out."

"I think I see where this is going," Tim said.

"I get back from the assignment, and my 4Runner is gone. Standing in its place is a new Toyota Truck."

"And that's why you don't want the truck."

"I mean, it was a nice truck," Terry said. "Four-wheel drive, V6, all the good options, none of the bullshit. She thought I'd be like Marty McFly seeing that thing in the garage. And like I said, it was nice. It was something I could drive to work without catching too much shit. So I put on a happy face and gushed about how wonderful it was."

"But really, you just wanted your crappy old 4Runner back," Tim said.

"Naturally," Terry said. "I even went to the dealer, tried to undo it. But they'd already sold off the 4Runner to an auction house. It was gone forever."

"So, what you got there?" Tim asked, pointing to the newspaper sitting on the bar in front of Terry. It was folded open to the classifieds, cars for sale.

"I'm looking for the cheapest piece of shit I can find that still actually runs," Terry said. "Some really good prospects here. I'm not budging over five hundred bucks. Hey, check out this '65 Impala for $275. I bet I could talk him down to $200."

Tim groaned.

"Ah, Jesus, man," Tim said. "You're not really gonna buy some clapped-out junker, are you?"

"All I can afford, anyway," Terry said. "And I need a new ride."

"Why do I see myself becoming your taxi service in the near future?"

"Because you get a free car with unlimited mileage as a perk of your profession?" Terry said, hopefully.

Tim gave him a stare.

"Anyway, that's still not quite the end of the story," Terry said.

"I think I'll stick with the short version next time," Tim said.

Terry ignored him.

"The day I came home, found her with that shitbag Chase, guess what was in the driveway."

"A fucking Porsche?" Tim guessed.

"A fucking Porsche," Terry said. "The exact same kind of fucking Porsche she'd tried to give me, same color and everything. And then today, just like that, it clicked. I made the connection. She bought me the same kind of car owned by the guy she'd been fucking on the side the entire time we were together. She bought me the same car as that dickface so it wouldn't look suspicious to the neighbors when he stopped by for a nooner."

"Guess he wasn't willing to drive a beat-up old Toyota," Tim said.

8

That Night

Terry was pulled from a fitful sleep aboard *Easy Goer*. He wasn't sure what woke him up. Then he heard it. It sounded like one of the dock carts, like big wheelbarrows, people used to bring stuff out to and from their boats, rolling along the ribbed surface of the ramp leading down to the floating dock.

He heard more shuffling around out there, and eventually the sound of a boat pulling out of a nearby slip. He didn't know what time it was, only that it was not light out yet. He caught a faint whiff of something bad, but it didn't linger. Not thinking much of it, he went back to sleep.

9

New Ride, New Job

Terry woke up the next morning with just the edge of a hangover lingering in his brain. He shook it off. He was resolved to get a new car today. He'd start with the Impala he'd seen in the paper last night, since it was within reasonable walking distance from the marina.

He hadn't slept well, the constant motion of the boat was somewhat unsettling. He was also vaguely aware of having been woken up sometime in the early-dawn hours by what sounded like someone coming back in and tying up in one of the slips near him. He wondered what the hell someone would be doing out that early, and assumed it was a fisherman. Those guys were insane.

He got out of his bunk and bundled up in navy blue sweats for the walk over to the marina's restroom building, grabbing his shower bag on the way. The morning was cold and gray, but that wasn't unusual in Ventura this time of year. June Gloom. It would burn off before lunchtime.

After a good, hot shower, the hangover receded a bit. Terry felt improved enough for a coffee, but there wasn't a coffee maker on *Easy Goer*, and he wasn't about to walk somewhere just to buy a cup of coffee. There was, however, a perfectly serviceable microwave, mugs, and a box of tea on board. He'd settle for the tea.

He drank his tea sitting in the cockpit of the boat, watching the gulls, swathed in a thick bathrobe on top of the sweats, and for a while he didn't think about anything at all. He saw a gray and white cat walking on the dock behind his boat. It looked young, not still a kitten, but not fully grown yet. He greeted the cat, who stopped for a moment and looked his way before moving on about his business. Terry went back to his tea.

Into this peaceful reverie stepped Wendy.

"Good morning, neighbor," she said, standing on the dock next to *Easy Goer*.

Terry snapped out of his trance and looked in her direction.

"Oh, good morning, Wendy." He raised his mug in her direction.

"Getting used to sleeping off-land yet?"

"I think I'd have a little trouble no matter where I'm sleeping, really," Terry said sheepishly. "Probably will take some time to adjust."

She was looking at him as if she expected more. Terry was at a loss. He didn't know what else to say. While it was nice that somebody wanted to have a casual conversation, he wasn't much up to sustaining one.

"Um, aren't you going to invite me on-board?" Wendy asked.

"Oh, sorry. Pardon my manners. I'm just learning the, uh, ropes on this whole boat thing. Please, come aboard."

Wendy smiled and ascended the short steps on the dock to board *Easy Goer*.

"Care for some tea?" he asked as she sat on the seat across from him in the boat's cockpit.

"Ah, no, thanks. I had coffee earlier. Too much caffeine doesn't work for me."

"So what do you have going on today?" Terry asked. He didn't really have much to say, but he didn't want her to leave.

"Well, my charter fell through for the day, so my plans are no longer valid. I am free. I'll probably just go to the Reach and bartend or work on the books." She looked to her left to take in the view across the harbor, then back at Terry. "What about you?"

"Today, I am going to buy a car," he said.

"You sound pretty sure of that."

"I am," he said. "I have very low standards."

This time she laughed.

"You might not want to advertise that," she said.

"Yeah, I don't plan on telling the seller."

"Not quite what I meant."

Terry let it fly over his head.

"So how are you going to get around to these cars you want to look at when you don't have a car now?" she asked.

"I was planning on walking, I'm not looking at anything more than a couple miles away."

"I mean, do you want to walk?" she asked. "Like, you need the exercise or something?"

"Not particularly, but it seems the obvious solution. Much cheaper than taking a bunch of cabs. Hell, the cab rides would probably cost me more than whatever car I'm buying."

"Terry ..." she started.

"Like I said, low standards."

"Do you want a ride?" she asked. "I'm not doing anything today. I could totally go with." Terry paused for a moment. It had never occurred to him to ask Wendy for a ride. They didn't really know each other, and Terry wasn't one to impose on his friends, let alone fresh acquaintances. Even taking Sheriff Baker up on the offer to use his sailboat as a temporary crash pad felt wrong to him. He felt bad, like he had manipulated her into asking.

"Oh, I'm sorry," he said. "I don't mean to be a sad sack, or want to make you feel sorry for me. It'll be OK. I can handle a little walking."

Wendy almost let it go, but decided not to.

"Terry, I'm offering because I want to," she said. "My plans fell through, I've got nothing to do, this would be something different. And you," she looked up and smiled at him again. "You need to learn how to let people in. It's OK to let people help you when you need help."

Terry's head was about as much of a mess as could be expected in his situation. He felt like he didn't know how to relate to anyone anymore, and anything connected to emotions just seemed like a bunch of wires got crossed somewhere. He didn't like the feeling. He was used to handling his own problems. He never felt the need to let people in before. To his way of thinking, that was needy, an imposition, the kind of thing that wore out friendships. Terry's philosophy was to ask as little as possible of the people in his life, and the world around him.

"It would be very nice to have your company. Thank you."

"Get dressed," Wendy said. "I'll be back in 15 minutes. Then we can go."

She got up, walked off the *Easy Goer*, and walked down the dock to her own boat. Terry watched her go, then got up and went below deck to change into real clothes. A pair of lightweight denim jeans, a plain gray t-shirt, and tan Sperrys was his ensemble for the day. He combed his hair again, now that it was drier, and decided to add a ballcap since he'd probably be outdoors longer than usual today.

Then he looked at himself and muttered, "This won't work."

When he and Mallory had been together, he had let her buy his clothes for him. He actually preferred to do his own shopping, but Mallory hated his wardrobe. Eventually he caved in and let her just do his shopping so he didn't have to listen to her criticism. But this meant that even though he was a t-shirt and jeans kind of guy, his jeans and t-shirts still had designer labels. Mallory had expensive tastes in jeans and t-shirts.

"This is no good," he said to no one in particular. "I look like I have too much money."

He took everything back off, put the sweat pants back on and found the cheap pair of flip- flops he bought the day before. Then he took his gray shirt, crumpled it up so it would wrinkle, and went up to wipe condensation from the deck with it.

Wendy returned just as Terry was climbing up the steps to the cockpit of *Easy Goer*.

"Ready?" she asked.

"Oh. Ready," he said, shrugging into the shirt quickly. He abandoned the deck-wiping idea. This was probably good enough. Wendy eyed his ensemble with something resembling suspicion, but didn't say anything about it.

Wendy drove an old squarebody GMC truck, looked to be from the late '70s. It was two-tone, blue with a silver inset down the side, and was beautifully well preserved.

"Wow, sweet truck," Terry said, upon climbing into the passenger side and settling on the wide, blue vinyl and plaid cloth bench seat.

"Thanks," she said. "It's not for sale." She turned and grinned at him. Terry noticed, not for the first time, that Wendy was a stunner. Especially when she smiled.

"I couldn't afford it anyway," he said. "Maybe someday."

"It's not a fucking Lamborghini, y'know," she said. "It's just an old truck. You could have two, if you wanted."

"I don't think you appreciate the price range I'm looking for," he replied. "But you'll see what I mean soon enough." She did see.

When they pulled up to the house with the '65 Impala in the driveway, Wendy almost refused to stop.

"That?" she asked, looking at the Impala wearing an expression of disgust.

Terry shrugged.

"Terry, low standards implies that there at least are standards."

He hopped out of the truck to check out the old Chevy. It was thoroughly beaten. At some point its original Tahitian Blue had been painted over with gray primer, from the look of it a long time ago. Terry leaned down to peek through the driver side window, then recoiled a couple inches.

"Stinks," he said.

The interior was in worse shape than the outside, springs poking through the upholstery of the stained and mismatched front and rear seats, loose wires visible hanging under the dashboard. "Smells like several cats pissed in it, and then it mildewed."

He looked over at Wendy, who hadn't gotten out of the truck.

"Yeah, let's get out of here," he said.

Next up was a battered 1973 Ford Torino sedan. It had started life as a light shade of baby-puke green, but there wasn't a single panel left on it that wasn't dented, scraped, and showing surface rust. The inside of this one reeked of stale beer and pot. Not wanting to have to explain that in a traffic stop, he moved on.

They looked at a few other beaters, each one somehow worse than the one before. The last stop was a tire shop on Thompson, where someone was selling a diseased-looking 1970 Buick Electra 225 sedan. It had been a handsome bronze color with a vinyl roof when it was new, but the Southern California sun had turned it into a chalky haze. The vinyl top had long ago rotted, and had been ripped off in strips, leaving little tufts of vinyl, adhesive and padding spattered across the roof. The hubcaps were missing, leaving bare black steel wheels.

"Here about the car?" asked a man in greasy coveralls. His name patch read "Rudy" in red script.

"Yeah," Terry said. He peeked in the interior, which looked to be in pretty good condition. "How much you asking?"

"Eight hundred," the man said. "It's been gone through mechanically. Brakes just rebuilt, new shocks. Original 455, only year they made the 455 with high compression. She's got headers, dual exhaust. I put a lumpy cam in it too, so she moves."

"Everything work, air conditioning, windows?" Terry asked.

"Yeah, she's mechanically perfect," the man said. "Just ugly as hell. Sucks down the gas, too."

Terry walked around the back of the car. The rear bumper was bent from what looked like a low-speed collision with something heavier than a '70 full-size Buick, whatever that may be. On the left side of the bumper, slightly faded and starting to crack, was the clincher. The sticker read: President Nixon. Now More Than Ever. It was a relic of the 1972 presidential campaign, the event that set Watergate in motion. Terry knew on seeing that that he had to have this car.

The man in the coveralls was going on. "It's got good tires, used, but about 60 percent tread left on them, and they all match. Got it at an estate sale. Must've sat outside for years. Only 53,000 miles, though."

It was true: Rudy had picked the Buick up at an estate sale. But he hadn't bought it. He was paid $75 to haul it away. A couple of weeks after that, he'd found an old Riviera Stage I with a cracked block in a pick-and-pull junkyard. He'd gone in on wheelbarrow day, and pulled the muscle car's heads, cam, intake manifold, and carburetor off the engine, and taken the 3.91 Positraction differential out of the axle. When he put those parts on the Electra, he'd cooked up a fairly potent sleeper. It was enough to dust off a new five-liter Mustang, at least. But Rudy liked building cars more than driving them, and now he was bored of the Electra and wanted to build something else.

Terry opened the driver's door and leaned in, inhaling cautiously. It had a slight, pleasant old-car aroma, not the malignant funk he was dreading.

"Will you take four hundred for it?" Terry asked.

"Five," Rudy replied.

Terry smiled and pulled a wad of bills out of his pocket. "Deal," he said, counting off five one hundred dollar bills. "How much gas you leave in it?"

"Got a full tank," the man said, pocketing the money and looking over one last time at the car. "Won't last you very long, though. Got a posi 3.91

in the rear end." He handed the keys over to Terry. "Rudy Santos, by the way."

"Thanks. Terry Cahill."

"Hey, if you ever need her worked on, you can bring her back here to me. I know her pretty well."

"Thanks again," Terry said.

Wendy looked over and rolled her eyes. Terry walked over to where she was standing.

"Well, that didn't take as long as I'd thought," he said. "If you're still free, how 'bout I take you out to lunch, to thank you for driving me around?"

"Save your money," she said, looking at Terry's new Buick. "Looks like you're going to need it to feed that whale you just bought. How about instead you follow me over to the Reach and lunch is on me?"

"Sounds good to me," Terry said.

Terry fired up the Electra and dropped the lever into Drive to follow Wendy back to the marina. The big 455 had a bit of a lope at idle, and a slightly louder, more rumbling voice than it had left the factory with. Most people would just assume that was a result of being an old hooptie with a rusted-out muffler. Terry appreciated the couch-like comfort of the bench seat in his faded luxury car. It drove him smoothly and without complaint to the marina's parking lot. In that short drive, Terry decided he liked the Buick.

Inside the Beam Reach Terry found Wendy sitting at the bar and chatting with the bartender. Terry joined her, sitting at the stool to her right.

"I know it's inconvenient, but it's the only day I can do it," the bartender was saying as she slid a Dos Equis in front of Wendy. She looked over at Terry.

"Schlitz, please," he said.

"Damn, Jody, I have a charter all day Tuesday," Wendy said. "I can't cancel it now. Probably lose more money than closing the Reach."

Jody set a cold mug and a can of Schlitz in front of Terry. He poured the can out into the chilled mug and took a deep pull off the beer.

"Look, when classes start up again, I'm going to have to go part-time anyway," Jody said. "You might as well look for someone to cover now."

Wendy looked over at Terry. "You need a job," she said. "You're not doing anything. You ever bartend?"

"I worked behind a bar for a couple semesters while I was in college," Terry said. "I make a decent martini and a damn fine margarita, but I don't know how to make those fancy tiki cocktails you do here."

"That's OK, about half of our customers just want a beer and a shot anyway, and you can take care of them. You won't be working alone, and I can teach you how to make the fancy rum drinks. Want a job? It could just be until you find something else. It'd really help me out."

"Yeah, sure," Terry said.

"Really?"

"Yeah, why not. Like you said, I need a job, and I'm not really doing anything else. Hell, it might even be fun."

"In that case, lunch really is on me," she said, smiling.

"Speaking of, do I get an employee discount?"

"You already get a discount for being my friend," she said. "And preferential treatment, too."

"Fair enough." Terry liked the sound of Wendy calling him her friend.

A new job and a new car, in one day, Terry thought. *Maybe starting over won't be all that bad.*

10

Seeking Justice

Vin Capriani sat in Sheriff Baker's office absent-mindedly playing with an unlit cigarette and looking across the desk between him and the sheriff. Baker had known about Vin before he'd ever become sheriff of Ventura County. People with reputations like his rarely escape the attention of law enforcement.

"I want justice for Brandon," Capriani said. "He's not just some hood, y'know. He's a good kid."

"I understand," replied Baker. "For what it's worth, I want justice for him too. It's just a matter of jurisdiction. Rincon Point straddles the county line, and it sounds like the assault happened on the Santa Barbara side."

"I knew you cops would play hot potato with this one ..." Vin started.

"I'm still looking into it, Mr. Capriani," Baker said. "I just need you to understand that this investigation could get complicated, and justice could take a long time. If it didn't happen in my county, I'll have to give what I have over to Santa Barbara."

"I want to handle this all nice and legal, you understand? Because of my son. He'd want it that way. But I am not a patient man, sheriff. And I know that sheriff over in Santa Barbara. I don't trust his ass." It wasn't the first time Baker had heard unflattering things about his counterpart in the county north of his.

"You could always hire a private investigator. They don't have the same limitations on jurisdiction."

"Yeah? You know someone you trust?"

Baker gave a thin smile. "I think so ..."

• • •

Brandon Capriani was not in the same line of work as his father. He was strictly legit, a college student and a surfer. He was not the most ambitious kid, his main aspiration being having a good time, but overall Vin was right about his son. He was a decent guy.

His father had wanted to name him Brando, after the actor, but the child's mother would not have it. She wanted her son to have a normal, American-sounding name. Brandon was the compromise they reached, and as he grew up his father realized that his wife had known best. It was clear from pretty early on that Brandon did not possess the kind of personality needed to follow in his father's footsteps. But Vin loved his only son more than anything, and even felt relieved that he was not cut out for the criminal lifestyle.

The attack that put Brandon in a hospital bed happened on a beach called Rincon Point. It was a spot famous among surfers for its waves. It was not the most beautiful beach in the area, being a narrow strip between PCH and the coastline that was frequently more rock than sand, and it wasn't popular with sunbathers or tourists. Rincon Point was pretty much only good for surfing. Brandon hadn't surfed there yet, and had wanted to check it out when he was visiting home during the summer break from college. The problem was that over the years, a gang of violent surfers calling themselves the Santa Barbara Boys had claimed the beach as their own.

The Santa Barbara Boys terrorized anyone they saw trying to surf "their" beach. Their tactics included assault and battery, as well as vandalism. Several would-be surfers had been beaten up and had their boards broken for the crime of visiting Rincon Point, and some of them had even gone back to their cars to find their tires slashed. Nobody had ever been prosecuted, or even arrested, for these attacks. The Santa Barbara Boys had become brazen in the absence of any repercussions for their poor behavior, and had even constructed a stone structure on the beach that they called their clubhouse. It was more of a pile of rocks, but regardless of what they called it, it was also illegal. Nobody seemed interested in doing anything about it, though.

Though these incidents had been publicized from time to time locally, Brandon did not get newspapers from California while he was in college back east. He wasn't entirely ignorant of the situation, but had vastly underestimated its seriousness. Every surfer had encountered aggressive assholes trying to defend their turf at some point, and Brandon assumed it was just more of the same.

But when Brandon and his friend Dave Sims tried surfing at Rincon, they soon learned that these were no ordinary assholes. Instead of the usual minor intimidation tactics, the four members of the Santa Barbara Boys they encountered went straight to assault. They walked right up to the two strangers, and beat the shit out of them. Brandon fell backward and hit his head on one of the large stones on the beach. Sims was lucky to get out with mostly just bruises and a couple of cracked ribs. The assault ended abruptly when Brandon was knocked out in the fall, blood oozing from the back of his head and spreading on the rock beneath it.

Sims had run to the nearest phone, which turned out to be a CHP call box on PCH. He got an ambulance sent out for his friend, and went back to the beach to wait with him. He wasn't sure which he felt more: terror or fury. He felt plenty of both, but as time went on the fury definitely won out.

11

Hanging On

In another hospital room, in another city, another man lied in a hospital bed with tubes and IVs connected to him. Jon-Jon was out cold on as heavy a dose of morphine as the doctors at St. Francis dared allow him. He didn't particularly notice the missing half of his leg yet.

Immediately after the shark attack, one of the uninjured Santa Barbara Boys ran to PCH looking for a phone, only to find a vandalized CHP call box. The cable to the handset had been cleanly severed with a pair of bolt cutters. He ran back to the beach in a panic, not knowing what to do. One of the other Boys ran out to PCH and flagged down a passing trucker. The trucker used his CB radio to call in the emergency. If it hadn't been for that outdated mode of communication, Jon-Jon would have bled out on the beach.

Jon-Jon had been visited by friends, family, and some of his fellow Santa Barbara Boys earlier in the day, but visiting hours were long over now and it was late at night. He had been among the largest and most physically aggressive of the gang, responsible for 47 assaults resulting in injury over the years. Now he was barely alive.

The man who entered his room was dressed in green scrubs, wearing latex gloves, a surgical mask and cap, paper booties covering his shoes. To anyone who happened to observe, he thought he would have looked like he belonged in the hospital, although it was a bit odd for a doctor to be checking in on Jon-Jon at this hour. He hadn't brought a weapon with him, no vial of poison and a needle. The pillow on the unoccupied bed next to Jon-Jon's would work well enough.

There was no beeping heart monitor to flatline and give the man away as he slipped back into the hallway. He was convinced he had left nothing behind as evidence except a dead Jon-Jon.

12

An Interesting Offer

Terry woke up to his pager beeping. It was not his preferred way to start a day. He grumbled to himself for a few seconds before reaching for the obnoxious little device and checking it to find he had not one, but two pages. He recognized both of the numbers.

The first was Desmond's office. Terry figured he probably already knew what that one was about. The second was from Sheriff Baker. He assumed that the callback to Tim would be the shorter of the two, and opted to make that call first.

He went through his morning routine of putting on sweats and a robe, grabbing his shower bag, and heading over to the marina's bathroom to get prepared for the day. After a shower, a shave, and a mug of tea on the deck of *Easy Goer*, he was ready to walk over to the payphone outside the Beam Reach to return the calls.

Tim was in his office and answered on the second ring.

"Good morning, sheriff. It's Terry."

"Hey, Terry," Tim said. "Glad you got back to me. I'm kinda busy right now, but I was thinking I'd come by this evening to run something by you. Can you meet me at the Reach tonight?"

"Yeah, I'll be there from 6 to close. Come on by." He was curious about what the sheriff wanted to talk about. *Guess I'll find out tonight,* he thought.

"OK, good. I'll see you then. I gotta run."

"All right, see you then, sheriff." Terry hung up and dialed Desmond's office.

"Terry, so good of you to call back," Desmond said.

"Anytime, Des. What can I do for you?"

"Actually, I was hoping you could come by my office to talk about it."

"Yeah, sure. What time is good?"

"Say, right after lunch? I've got an hour free at 1:30."

"OK, I'll see you then."

"Thanks, Terry. I'll see you soon."

Terry hung up the phone and looked at his watch, a beat-up old analog Timex on its second replacement band, and saw that it was just after 10 a.m. He had some time to kill before his appointment with Desmond. He decided to run a couple of errands.

Terry unlocked his Buick and dropped down onto the cushy bench seat. The car fired almost as soon as he turned the key, coughing to life with a rumble that quickly smoothed out to a low-pitched rhythmic hum through the dual exhaust and a faint constant hiss from the big 4-barrel Q-jet under the hood. He let the big iron block warm up for a few minutes before dropping the lever into Reverse and feeling the car 'thunk' into gear, the body shifting its weight on the suspension as the TH400 dumped the 455's considerable torque at idle into the equation.

He let off the brake and eased out of his parking spot, then 'thunked' into Drive and cruised out of the parking lot floating on a cloud of pillowy suspension, numb, effortless steering, and seemingly inexhaustible reserves of torque. Everything about driving the car required a light touch. You could steer it all day with just one finger if you wanted to. The brake pedal needed merely the suggestion of being used to produce unpleasantly jerky stops, and even the thought of using more than the first third of throttle travel would convert the rear tires into foul-smelling smoke. It weighed 4,500 lbs., all of the controls were hilariously overboosted and sensitive, and the suspension was as firm as marshmallow fluff. And it had at least 500 ft-lbs. of torque.

His first stop was the Kmart on Victoria Avenue. He needed a new pair of sneakers and some t-shirts and undies. Terry loved Kmart. It was probably his favorite store. Sears was OK, too. But Kmart was better, usually had slightly cheaper prices. In the days before he married Mallory Getz, he was fond of saying that if he couldn't find something at Kmart, he probably didn't need it anyway.

Mallory, on the other hand, hated Kmart, and refused to be seen in one. Shopping at Kmart was one of the things he'd missed while living with her. It felt good to be among the familiar sights and smells of the bargain chain, to hear the announcement of a Blue Light Special over the public address. He picked out a cheap pair of sneakers and a couple of 3-packs of plain t-shirts.

While browsing the store, he made an impulse purchase in the music section, something rare for him. He put three cassettes in his cart along with the shirts and shoes: Roger Miller's "The 3rd Time Around," Marty Robbins's "Adios Amigo," and Chet Atkins's "Chet Atkins in Hollywood." He had left all his music behind when he left Mallory, most of his tape collection sitting in a case under the seat of the Toyota truck he used to drive. One of the previous owners of his current Buick had installed a Craig stereo with a built-in tape deck at some point over the years, probably sometime in the last decade. It wasn't always possible to get good reception from radio stations broadcasting from Los Angeles up in Ventura County, as the mountains sometimes got in the way, and Terry liked to listen to music as he drove.

He checked out at the cashier stand, and bought a copy of the day's *Los Angeles Times* from a dispenser in front of the store on his way out. With his purchases in hand, he hopped back in the Buick and headed up Victoria, then took Telephone Road to cut over to Main Street. His next stop was a laundromat on Main. He had brought a bag of clothes to wash along with the stuff he'd just bought.

Terry fed the change machine in the laundromat a $5 bill and put his clothes, old and new, in a couple of washing machines. At this time of day, the laundromat was almost deserted, and he found a seat near the machines he was using and opened up the newspaper. He spent the next hour and a half reading the paper while waiting on his clothes.

It was lunchtime by the time Terry was done at the laundromat, and his stomach was awake enough to announce its emptiness. There was a Shakey's Pizza Parlor one street over on Santa Clara Street, and he drove there to grab a bite. He had a couple of slices of pepperoni and washed them down with a frosty mug of Stroh's. It was blissful.

With lunch finished, he got back in the Buick, made a quick stop at the marina to drop off his new clothes on *Easy Goer* and change into his new sneakers and a freshly clean t-shirt, and then drove up the 101 to Desmond's office in Santa Barbara, listening to the Marty Robbins tape on the way. He made it with a few minutes to spare. With the 3.91 gears in the axle, the big Buick didn't like going much over 65 mph on the freeway. The 455 was turning just over 3,000 rpm at that speed, and really sucking down the gas in the process.

Desmond's secretary greeted Terry as he walked in. Terry had only been there a couple of times before, but she remembered his name and offered him coffee, which he accepted. He hadn't had a cup of coffee since leaving his former life behind, and while tea was nice every now and then, it wasn't the same. He savored the warm black liquid in its styrofoam cup.

Desmond came out to greet Terry, and escorted him back to his office. He was a compact man in his mid-sixties with curly gray hair, closely cropped, and the same olive complexion as his daughter. He kept himself in shape, and had a firm handshake, which he offered Terry upon seeing him.

His office was a large space on a corner, with windows looking out on meticulously landscaped and manicured grounds that would have put some PGA golf courses to shame. The office wasn't the stereotypical lawyer's suite, dark with wood paneling and shelves lined with leather-bound books. It was bright, clean, stark, and, in the mid '50s — when Desmond started his law firm — would have been considered impressively "modern." The furniture, a combination of teak, anodized aluminum, and leather, had a distinctly Scandinavian influence. On his desk sat an object most people wouldn't recognize, a metal contraption covered in lenses and dials, and with cloth-wrapped wires coming off it. It was a WWII-era Norden bombsight.

"Thank you for coming all the way up here," Desmond said. "I would have come down to see you, but I didn't have enough time to drive to Ventura and back. I hope you understand."

Terry shrugged. "It's no bother for me," he said. "I have a little more time on my hands than you do for the time being. So what's up, Des?"

"I wanted to get some background out of the way on the wrongful termination suit we'll be filing against your former employer. I have my people doing research on the publisher and the paper itself, of course, but I need to get your story from you, as well." Desmond paused for a moment. Terry could tell he was struggling with something.

"But before we get into that," Desmond continued, "I want to ask you a personal favor."

Terry felt a sinking feeling in his gut. "What can I help you with, Des?" he asked.

"Please hold off for a little while on filing the divorce papers. For Mallory's sake."

"Des, I'd just be putting off the inevitable. The divorce is happening."

"I realize that, and I'm not trying to talk you out of it. But please, just wait a few weeks. Maybe a couple of months. Terry, I'm really worried about her. I know you want to be free, and maybe I don't even blame you after what you've been through. But I'm asking, not only as her father, but as your friend: Do you want to be divorced, or do you want to be a widower?"

The words hit Terry hard. "She's that bad?" he asked quietly.

"I'm her dad. Maybe I worry too much. But maybe I don't worry enough, you know?"

"Yeah, I think I do."

"She's never been, how can I put this, a particularly stable person. When you two were together, that was the most grounded I ever saw her. It's a big adjustment for her, you leaving, and she's taking it hard. Particularly because she thinks it's all her fault. I'm not asking you to move back in with her. Just, please, don't serve her with papers right away."

"You know, she may need help," Terry said. "Like, professional help. I mean, I don't want anything to happen to her either. Once upon a time, I loved her very much. I don't want any harm to come to her."

"We're looking into that."

"I guess what I'm saying is, if it would help, and she's in therapy, I could be a part of that. If it would help her to have me there, in that setting."

"Thank you, Terry. That means a lot to me."

"Yeah, you're welcome. I mean, you don't have to thank me for that."

Desmond looked down at Terry's left hand, and a slight smile crossed his face. "I notice you're still wearing your ring," he said.

Terry looked down himself and saw the shiny gold band on his ring finger. He hadn't thought about it. He'd only taken the ring off a handful of times since getting married. Now he wondered why he hadn't taken it off after leaving.

"I guess technically I'm still married," Terry said.

"Yes. I guess technically you are." Desmond smiled.

They spent the next few minutes talking about Terry's experience at the *Monitor*, and Des ran out of questions, for this session at least, just as 2:30 rolled around. Terry got up to leave, and Desmond joined him.

"Let me walk you out to your car," Desmond said. "I need to stretch my legs and get some air."

They walked out to the parking lot together. Desmond looked amused when he saw Terry's Electra.

"So that's how you're getting around these days," Des said. "Mallory said you left the truck behind."

Terry looked sheepish. "The truck wasn't really mine," he said. "I mean, I didn't buy it with my money." Desmond didn't argue the point.

"Fine cars, these were. 1970?" Terry nodded. "I had one, back when they were new. Possibly the most comfortable car I ever owned. Effortless acceleration."

"I thought you were an Oldsmobile man," Terry said.

"I go back and forth between them and Buicks," Des replied.

"And a Porsche."

"Ugh, don't remind me," Des laughed. "What am I, a nice Jewish boy, doing with a Nazi car like that?" he said, shaking his head. "It's embarrassing. I'm from a generation that remembers such things. My daughter, not so much. I know, I should have gotten it out of my system by now. I got my personal revenge in the nose of a B-17 over Germany many years ago. But I still hate being seen in that damn car. Some nights I dream about taking it to the junkyard and having it crushed while I watch."

"If you ever do that, I hope you'll invite me along."

"You'll be the first person I'll call. Hey, you like Toyotas. What do you think of those new Lexuses?" He was pointing at a black LS400 in the back of the parking lot.

"From what I've seen, they seem pretty solid. I think they're gonna give the Krauts a hell of a lot of trouble, especially if they can keep selling them at the prices they are now. Why? You thinking of something new?"

"I'm considering trading in my Ninety-Eight. Barely two years old, and I'm having problems with it." He sighed. "Buick and Oldsmobile don't make them like they used to anymore."

"I'm pretty happy with this Buick," Terry said.

"Of course you are."

"So, I know why you wouldn't buy a Benz, but what makes the Japanese any different in your eyes?"

"Two things: Hiroshima, and Nagasaki. I figure those books have been balanced."

They said their goodbyes, and Terry pointed his hooptie south on the 101 for the return trip to the Ventura marina.

• • •

Sheriff Baker walked into the Beam Reach and was surprised to find Terry on the other side of the bar, washing glasses. The place was nearly deserted, but it was early in the evening yet, and on a weekday.

"Wendy making you wash dishes to pay off your tab?" Tim asked.

"Ha, no," Terry said. "I am once again gainfully employed."

"Bartending at the Reach? That's really your next career move?"

"It's better than nothing, and nothing is what I had two days ago," Terry replied. "I'm planning to sue the *Monitor* for firing me. After that gets out, win or lose, I'll never get a job in journalism again. The industry tends to love whistleblowers, until the whistle is blown on one of their own."

"They sound kinda like cops. Circle the wagons, all that."

"From what I've seen of the world, people are pretty much all the same, regardless of what they do." He considered. "Hell, this might be a better job than reporting anyway."

"Speaking of," Tim started. Terry put down the glass he was drying and looked at his friend the sheriff. "How would you like the chance to get back into some investigative work?"

Terry turned around, reached down into the beer bin and popped a Dos Equis. He stuffed a lime wedge in the mouth of the bottle and set it on the bar in front of Tim.

"What kind of investigative work?" Terry asked.

"I've got a case, but I think it'll end up not being my case," Tim began. He told Terry the story of Brandon Capriani's beating at the beach, and how he was getting pressure from Vin Capriani to investigate.

"Vin Capriani?" Terry asked. "*The* Vin Capriani? Connected guy? Suspected mob boss?"

"You'd actually be working for him," Tim said. "I'm just making the arrangement for him. Of course, I'll be doing my own investigation." The sheriff took a swig of beer. "But you have a knack for coming up with angles my guys don't always think of. It wouldn't hurt to run parallel investigations. And you don't have the same jurisdictional issues I do."

"Jurisdiction? I have no jurisdiction at all. Isn't it illegal for someone to pay me as a private investigator if I don't have a license?"

"Yes, for the most part. But it's totally legal for you to investigate as a freelance journalist writing up a story about violence on our beaches. And it is also legal for a publication to pay you an advance on such stories. Did you know that Capriani's investment holding company owns a majority stake in a company that runs a series of alternative weekly newspapers and other publications?"

"I was not aware of that," Terry said. "His name has come up in some things I've poked into, but I've never gotten anything I could print on the guy."

"He's smart, for a crook. And careful. I've tried to nail him before, but never had any more luck than you seem to have."

"Which brings me to another question: Why should I work for someone like him?"

The sheriff shrugged. "Everybody deserves justice. Even Vin Capriani. He's still a citizen, and he's still entitled to the protection of the law, just like anyone else. Besides, it's his son who's in a hospital right now, not Vin. His son is just a goofy surfer kid."

"Yeah, OK, but why isn't Vin just handling this with his own guys?"

"That's something I'd prefer not to happen," Tim said. "And he isn't, because the mob is long on muscle, but short on investigative savvy. They'd make a mess out of finding out who is responsible, and Vin's sharp enough to know that."

"You know he could want to use me as his stalking horse? Have me track the guys down, then have his goons do the muscle part."

"The thought had crossed my mind. But he knows I'm looking into it too. If he pulls something like that, I might just get the chance to hang his ass for it. I think he's too careful for that. I could be wrong, but my gut says he wants to handle this the legal way." He considered. "Mostly. I also expect you to share everything you learn with me first, so his goons won't have a head start."

Terry thought about the offer. It was an interesting problem the sheriff had brought to him. It did sound like a good story, the kind of thing he couldn't resist.

"OK, I'll do it. I mean, the bartending gig is only part-time anyway. I can do it in my time off."

"Great," Tim said, handing over Capriani's business card. "You can contact him tomorrow. Now, how about another beer?"

Terry popped another Dos Equis and slid it over to the sheriff.

"So, there's one more thing I need to tell you about this," Tim started. "There's this group calling themselves the Santa Barbara Boys. Bunch of surfer dickheads who think they own the beach. They're supposedly responsible for several assaults at Rincon, but not much has ever been done about them. I actually put them into the state's gang database. Got a pissed-off call from my counterpart in Santa Barbara about that one.

"Yeah?" Terry said.

"What I'm saying is, be careful. I have a feeling they might be, uh, protected somewhat up in Santa Barbara County."

"I can handle myself."

"Yeah, I know. Ex-military." The sheriff finished off his beer. "But before you go up to Rincon, if you go, I want you to call a friend of mine. He'll ride along."

He handed Terry a business card.

TAMBO Industries, VPBJJ
851 E. Front St., Ventura CA
Lance Thompssen
805.223.7737

13

Discovery

A nurse found Jonathan Abernathy dead during his 6:45 a.m. rounds at St. Francis. At first there wasn't much surprising about the discovery. Although the doctors and staff had done their best, Abernathy had been in deep shock and had lost a significant amount of blood. Everybody hoped he'd pull through, but everybody knew there was more than a chance that he wouldn't.

That was before the doctor came in and saw the rash developing on the dead man's face.

"Well, that's interesting," Dr. Susan Kreutz said to no one in particular as she bent over to get a closer look. It was faint, but there.

She went out to the nurse's desk and asked the duty nurse to call the police non-emergency line. Roughly an hour later a plainclothes deputy showed up at the hospital, asking for Dr. Kreutz. The doc met Detective Decker in Abernathy's room, the corpse having not been moved yet.

"I think you may want an autopsy performed on this man," Kreutz told Decker. "We can, of course, perform it here, or the ME may want it done in a county facility. That is why you're here. We felt it best to give you the option. But also, it's probably better if it's done sooner, and we're right here."

"It's fine if you want to do it," Decker said after thinking for a moment. It was a Saturday, and he knew the county ME was probably not going to be easy to get ahold of out on the links, and Kreutz was listed as an auxiliary ME with the county. Besides, if the hospital wanted to perform an autopsy, Decker knew all they needed was permission from the deceased's next of kin. He probably couldn't stop her, and he was curious himself. "You've done autopsies for us before. What makes you think we want one?"

Kreutz pointed to Abernathy's face. "The first clue is that rash that just started developing around his face. I suspect it is an allergic reaction."

Decker looked back down at the dead man lying in the hospital bed. Though most of his body was covered by a blanket, he couldn't help noticing the prodigious amount of hair that had grown on the man's shoulders.

"Why is that unusual?" Decker asked.

"Because everything we use here is hypoallergenic. It has to be. We can't take chances on something causing a severe reaction. So everything in here that would have touched his face should not be capable of causing this reaction. But something did, and I'd need to see an autopsy to be sure, but off the top of my head, I suspect it is a reaction to latex, as used in gloves. I checked his chart, and the allergy is noted."

Jon-Jon was indeed allergic to latex. He had used that fact primarily to avoid wearing condoms once the safe-sex era had began. Now it looked like his allergy might help point to foul play in his demise.

Kreutz pointed to Abernathy's eyes, and the skin around them, continuing. "There is some evidence of hemorrhaging around the eyes that can be indicative of suffocation. Again, I'd need an autopsy to know for sure. It's possible he just stopped breathing, or an airway was restricted due to an allergic reaction. But it's also possible that it's not. I just got kind of a hincky feel about this one."

Decker looked interested. "You mean petechial hemorrhaging?"

Kreutz was sure this was something Decker had picked up from TV, not actual police work. "Yes, basically. Petechial hemorrhaging is frequently associated with strangulation, however it can be caused by many kinds of trauma. It can even happen from coughing too hard. In this case, it is slight, and to me that suggests smothering more than strangulation. There are no other obvious marks on his body, aside from the shark damage."

"OK, cut him up," Decker said. "Let's see what you can come up with. Let's seal up this room now, too. It could be a crime scene. By the way, I'm gonna need to see your security camera footage from the few hours leading up to you discovering Mr. Abernathy there."

"You'll have to talk to someone in operations about that," Kreutz said. "I'll see if I can point you in the right direction. Meanwhile, I'd like to get going on that autopsy, detective."

•••

Detective Decker ended up getting access to the view the security footage, but without evidence of an actual crime, like the completed autopsy results, hospital security would not allow him to remove the tapes from the premises. He started watching the tapes in fast forward. He was looking for someone who shouldn't be there, but not having any luck. The head of hospital security hovered around in the room with him, which irked Decker, but he let it go.

Decker knew he could end up spending hours doing this for nothing, but he also didn't have all that much to do as a Santa Barbara cop, nothing as interesting as a possible murder investigation, anyway. So he kept watching the tapes. The views covered the main hallway on each floor, near the elevators, and the entrances and exits on the ground floor. He had lost track of time when Dr. Kreutz came and found him. Decker paused the video to talk to the doc.

"It's definitely murder by suffocation," Kreutz said by way of greeting. "Don't have the lab work yet on the rash, but I'll bet it's a reaction to latex." Kreutz trailed off while looking at the screen Decker had paused. It showed a man dressed in scrubs, a surgeon's mask, and full gear walking out the hospital's back entrance.

"Latex gloves. I believe that's your murderer, right there," Kreutz said, pointing at the screen.

Decker didn't see it. Kreutz pulled a glove from the pocket of her scrubs and showed it to Decker. It was purple.

"Nitrile," Kreutz said. "Completely hypoallergenic. Everybody here uses them, and nothing else."

Though the security footage was in black and white, the doctor on the screen in the paused image had gloves that looked white. They definitely were not a darkish color, like the glove Kreutz just showed him.

"That guy is not wearing our gloves," Kreutz continued. I can't tell you just from the video that those are latex, but they're not what we use."

Decker turned back to the head of hospital security again.

"I'm going to need you to let me take these tapes now," Decker said. "I can get a court order, but please don't make me waste time doing it."

The head of security looked briefly at Dr. Kreutz, who nodded OK, then relented.

14

Night Work

Dave Sims was trying to be as quiet as he could loading his smelly cargo onto the boat. It was near 3 a.m., after that bar at the marina had closed, and a time when as few people were awake and about as could be expected in the harbor area. This window of opportunity, to be able to sneak in and out, was short.

He'd have three hours at best, he knew from experience, to get the night's work done and tie the boat back up in its slip without being observed. It wasn't unusual for boaters to go out at 6 a.m., but it was fairly unusual for them to be coming back in at that time. Unusual enough to be noticed, maybe even commented on. He dared not leave sooner due to the late-night crowd at the bar.

The only problem was that the lobster cages he was loading onto the boat were heavy on their own, and filled with a severed pig's head each, purchased from a local butcher and left to ripen in Sims's parents' back yard for a few days, too heavy for him to carry far. He had to use a dock cart, and the cart made some noise as its hard plastic front wheel rolled along the textured surface of the dock. It was unavoidable, but Sims deemed it an acceptable risk.

After he'd loaded the boat, he untied the cleat hitches holding the boat in its slip, and used an electric trolling motor to ease out of the harbor, again, hoping not to make noise. Some people slept on the boats tied up here, and he didn't want to draw attention.

The boat was a 32-foot Chris-Craft cabin cruiser belonging to his parents, who rarely took it out. Dave had a key, and permission to use it whenever he wanted. He even had a credit card billed to his parents that he could use for gas. He used to take his friends out when the waves weren't good for surfing but the weather too nice not to be on the water. Brandon Capriani had been one of those friends.

Once safely out of the harbor, he fired up the inboard main engine, and set a course north, the Mercury Marine V8 giving a muted roar as it pushed the boat up to 28 knots.

Though he was young, Sims was already an experienced boater, and knew the shoals and sandbars near the harbor area. He also knew how to read the surface of the water. Navigating at night and with slight marine layer forming would be challenging to most, but Sims, though careful, knew what he was doing. Just in case, he made sure the radar was working too, and kept his eye on it.

He reached his destination about 100 yards offshore of Rincon Point less than an hour later, cut the motor and let the boat drift. He didn't bother with dropping an anchor, as he'd be out of here soon enough. Besides, the drift would help with distributing his cargo. The first couple of times he'd done this, he had simply dumped buckets of chum over the side. The results had proven unsatisfactory, and he figured out quickly that he needed a way to keep the putrefying meat close enough to the shore to attract what he thought of as his new friends.

The first lobster cage fell into the water with a splash and immediately disappeared below the waves. The second soon joined it, along with the six other cages deposited on previous nights. Sims smiled at the moonlit surface.

He restarted the inboard, and set a course back to the Ventura Marina.

15

Chomp

It was another one of those June mornings on the coast that an out-of-stater would mistake for December. The sky was obscured by a thick marine layer, and the air had a chill that would prompt most people to reach for a sweater. Rincon Point beach, however, was not deserted.

Most surfers considered a shark attack as one of those remote possibilities much like being struck by lightning. It wasn't something they worried about happening, and for the most part they were right. Shark attacks on humans were exceedingly rare. Statistically, one has a better chance of winning the lottery.

So it wasn't out of character that just the day after Jon-Jon the surfer had been found dead in his hospital bed with half of one of his legs being digested into shark shit, Rincon Point beach was populated with surfers again. Santa Barbara Boys, friends of Jon-Jon. They intended to surf in celebration of his memory.

However, being early on a Sunday morning, there were only four of them. They had changed into their wetsuits and were charging into the water, not really considering any danger. Jon-Jon's attack had been a freak thing, right? There wouldn't be another shark attack at Rincon for the next 50 years.

At least, that's what they all thought.

The first indication that they had miscalculated was when Shane Larson was bitten in half along with his surfboard by a 17-foot adult Great White. He didn't even have time to scream. He just disappeared under a bloody foam, then parts of him resurfaced.

The other three Santa Barbara Boys would have jumped out of the water and run for shore if they could have. Seeing as they couldn't, two more of them were bitten, One lost his entire left arm to the same adult shark that had bitten their friend in half. The other had a deep gash in his right leg from a juvenile shark.

Kerry Kirkham was the lucky one. He made it to the beach without a scratch.

If he had been in his patrol car instead of his personal vehicle, he could have used the radio to call for help.

16

The Interview

Terry had spent the entire weekend working at the Beam Reach, drinking, and sleeping off hangovers on *Easy Goer*. At least the booze was free now. So was food, if he ate all his meals at the Reach. His stomach didn't like the idea of another grease-bomb of a burger, and not much else on the menu was palatable. He figured he'd probably be paying for his next couple of meals.

Now it was Monday morning, and Terry was starting his day by picking up a copy of the latest *LA Times* and brewing a mug of tea. He scanned the paper and found a story about another shark attack at Rincon. This one had apparently been fatal. He put the paper down without reading it.

Terry wanted to get to work on the Capriani thing the sheriff had dropped on him. He went to the Reach, let himself in and called the number Tim had given him and a gruff-sounding man answered.

"Vin," the voice on the other end of the line said.

Terry hadn't expected the man himself to answer. He thought he would get a secretary of sorts, some kind of a gatekeeper.

"Mr. Capriani, my name is Terry Cahill. Sheriff Baker referred me to you, said you might be interested in hiring me to write an investigative story. Is this a bad time?"

"No, no," Capriani said. "Glad you contacted me. I was gettin' worried you'd flake on me over the weekend when you didn't call."

"Sorry, Mr. Capriani," Terry said. "I had some other things to take care of over the weekend. Wanted to make sure I wasn't occupied with that stuff when I talked to you." It was bullshit, but fuck it. Terry wasn't even sure he wanted to work for a hood like Capriani, regardless of what the sheriff said about justice. He'd already worked for people he didn't like or trust much, and the experience had recently ended poorly for him. He wasn't eager to start that cycle anew.

"I understand," Capriani said. "Look, why don't we meet in person, talk this over."

"Yes, that's a good idea. Where would you like to meet?"

Capriani gave him the address and added, "And hey, call me Vin, OK."

"No problem, Vin. An hour from now good?"

"Better make it an hour and a half, kid. I'll see you then."

Terry hung up the phone at the Reach and picked up his shower bag from the bar. The place was closed, but Terry had a key now that he worked at the joint. He didn't go in frequently when the place wasn't open, but *Easy Goer* didn't have a phone on board, and he didn't feel like keeping a sack of quarters around to use a payphone every time he needed to make a call. And his calls were local. They wouldn't cost the bar anything.

He went out and locked the place back up, then walked over to the marina restroom building nearest to *Easy Goer.* It took him less than 15 minutes to get a shower and a shave before heading to the boat for the day's clothes and a mug of tea. He picked the newspaper back up to give it a more thorough read.

He was browsing the sections when he came back to the second story about sharks attacking surfers, and noticed it happened on the same beach as last time. *Huh, Rincon again?* he thought. *Man, what is going on with that place? Sharks in the water, dickheads on the beach.*

The story also made mention of a surfer by the name of Jonathan Abernathy who died in the hospital after losing his leg in the attack just days before. He had a feeling he would need to check that beach out in the course of investigating his story, and made a mental note to stay out of the water.

He was sitting in the cockpit of the boat with the newspaper in his lap, dressed in jeans and a long-sleeve blue and green striped polo shirt with boat shoes and no socks, nursing a mug of tea and staring out into the June Gloom when he saw a familiar face. The gray and white cat from the other day came strolling along the dock, his nose high in the air, eyes squinting in the direction of the sun, obscured though it was by the fog in the air. He looked like he was enjoying the morning.

"Hi, kitty," Terry said without expecting a response.

The cat stopped on the dock near the stern of *Easy Goer,* looked at Terry thoughtfully for a second, and meowed. Terry figured it'd be rude not to continue the conversation now that he had the cat's attention.

"Yeah, I like the mornings too," he said to the cat. "The day is full of promise. It's all yet to come." *Even a hangover and stories about sharks eating people can't bring me down,* he thought.

The cat seemed to think about that too, then meowed again. He sat down and started licking one of his front paws nonchalantly.

"I wonder if you live on one of the boats around here," Terry said. The cat kept bathing himself until a passing gull caught his eye. He looked at Terry again before he headed off down toward the end of the dock.

Terry finished off his tea, washed out his mug, left the paper on the galley counter, and made sure *Easy Goer* was ship-shape before locking the boat up and walking up the dock to shore, carrying a trash bag with him which was deposited in one of the two large bins next to the marina's dock gate. Before exiting through the gate, he checked his pocket for the sheriff's keyring. He didn't need the keys to get out of the dock, but he'd need them to get back to the boat. It wasn't something he wanted to leave without.

Parked at the curb of the vast parking lot, the Buick looked somewhat out of place. It's not that the marina's parking lot was full of luxury cars any more than its slips were full of yachts. But most of the vehicles in the sparsely populated lot said 'middle class.' Terry's Electra said, 'A bum lived in this car before moving on to a better address.' The Buick was comically huge compared to modern cars. He noticed a black sedan, a new Lexus LS400 parked a couple of spaces away, and his Electra dwarfed the new luxury car.

The address Vin had given him turned out to be a deserted-looking industrial building made of bare corrugated metal, situated on the corner of Junipero Street and East Thompson Boulevard. Terry parked the Buick in the small lot on the Junipero side of the building.

A short, youngish man with slicked back hair opened the door for Terry. "He's waiting for you. Back there." He nodded toward an office to the left.

"Thanks," Terry said, walking over to the door. He knocked.

"Come in," came the response from the other side of the door. Terry went in. "Have a seat."

Terry looked at the man behind the desk. Vin Capriani hadn't bothered to stand up. He was a large man, barrel-shaped, but not as tall as Terry. He wore nice clothes that fit as if they and been tailored for him, which they had. His fingernails were manicured and buffed to a high shine, and every detail of his grooming was technically perfect, at least as far as Terry could observe. Yet there was something rough about his edges. He didn't look like someone who was born to wear those clothes. He looked like someone who was wearing an impeccable uniform.

Terry sat down in a chair across from Vin, on the other side of his desk. Vin reached for a small box on his desk, pulled out a cigarette, and lit it with a gold lighter that made a distinct 'click' sound. He blew out the first drag over toward the corner of his office.

"My son is a good kid," Vin began. "Whatever you may think of me ..." he trailed off. His voice was similar to his appearance: He sounded smooth and refined, but his language and the way he used it revealed something crass about him hiding beneath the veneer of refinement. "My son is just a college student. All he really wants to do is have a good time."

"Nothing wrong with that," Terry offered. He felt like he was there to listen more than talk at the moment.

"It'd be one thing if he just got his ass kicked," Vin continued. "I'd be pissed off, but, you know, shit like that happens sometimes. But these fuckers ... I don't know if I'll ever get my son back. You know, all the way back?"

Terry couldn't help but feel sorry for Vin, and his son too, he supposed. It really wasn't fair what had happened to him.

"Anyway, I want the cocksuckers who did this brought to justice," Vin said. "And I want it done all legal. Now, the sheriff told me that you've written stories that have exposed crimes, actually gotten people busted. Is that right?"

"Yeah," Terry said. "I worked the cops 'n courts beat for three years. In that time, I exposed a few things, and sometimes people even went down for them. Not always, though."

"But you'd be willing to write one again, right? Especially if it was a good one?"

"Sure, it's what I do." Terry had a hunch, and played it. "Hey, Vin, do you mind showing me a copy of the publication you plan to publish this in? I mean, if we do go to press?"

Vin cracked a smile and blew out more cigarette smoke. "Sure thing, kid," he said, reaching into a desk drawer. He pulled out a glossy looking magazine and tossed it across the desk at Terry, who caught it without much effort.

Tail Magazine? Terry thought. He wondered if the groan he felt was audible. He'd be writing possibly the last story of his career for a skin-rag. It was not the capstone for which he had hoped.

"Do you mind if I use a pen name?" Terry asked, holding up the magazine.

"Whaddya got in mind?" Capriani asked.

"Dack Rockford," Terry replied deadpan.

Vin laughed. "Jesus Christ, kid. That's the porniest name I've ever heard, and I'm a fucking pornographer."

"I know," Terry said. "I'm reserving the name for myself in case I have to fall back on a second career option. I'm hoping you'll give me an audition if it comes to that."

Capriani stopped laughing for a moment and looked at Terry. He wasn't sure if he was just being a smartass, or if he was making fun of him. He let it go and started laughing again. Terry felt a slight chill. Capriani stopped laughing again.

"Look," Vin said. "I know you like to fuck around, crack jokes and shit. But I'm serious as fuck about bringing the guys who did this to justice, OK? I want you to remember that they put a totally innocent guy in a fucking coma. They'll probably do it again to someone else."

Terry looked Vin in the eye. It was his turn to pause and consider, fixing the other man in his gaze for a moment.

"I do not tolerate bullies very well, Vin," Terry began. This time Vin sensed it was time to sit back and listen himself. "When I was young, around 13, I wanted to fit in. I was an Army brat, moved around the country every couple of years, never got to stay in one place or keep any friends for very long. It was rough. As a kid, you want to belong, but you're never around anywhere long enough to get more than a taste.

"So I'm just becoming a teenager. I'm enrolled in a new school again for the start of middle school. I'm in this podunk town in Indiana, like 200 kids in the whole school, and there's this one kid everybody picks on.

I mean, there are the normal geeks and nerds and whatnot, but this kid is everyone's punching bag. Even the other unpopular kids shat all over this poor kid. Turns out, he was autistic."

"You mean like that 'Rain Man' movie?" Vin asked.

"Yeah, like that," Terry said. "Not quite as severe, but somewhere on that same spectrum. Anyway, one day, some kids were picking on him, his name was Curtis, and I decided I'd join in. As Curtis was getting ready to sit down, I pulled his chair out from behind him. He fell on the ground and started crying. Other kids started laughing, even the few who usually didn't pick on Curtis.

Vin lit another cigarette.

"Thing is, the teacher saw me do it," Terry said. "She busted my ass, reported me to the principal, and the school called my parents, told them what I did. So I go home, and my dad is waiting for me. We weren't very close, pops and I. I was mostly just afraid of him. He was a career Army guy, Special Forces and all that. He took it very seriously. I didn't feel like anything was worth taking seriously back then, except maybe trying to get laid.

"He came down on me hard. Didn't yell or hit me. Just gave me a pretty severe version of 'I'm disappointed in you.' Told me that every man in my family, going back as many generations as they could track, had served in the military. That every one of them signed up because they recognized that it was the duty of the strong to protect the weak, and that we were the strong.

"And then he told me that Curtis, the kid I'd picked on, was going to be my new best friend. It wasn't a suggestion. It was an order. I was to spend every minute outside of class with that kid. I'd eat lunch with him, sit next to him on the bus, walk with him in the halls, and stand up for him if anyone caused trouble. So I did it.

Vin tapped an ash into the ashtray, still looking at Terry.

"I made friends with him. Ate lunch with him. Rode on the bus with him. Soon enough, he forgot about how mean I was to him before, and we became real friends. I saw how wrong I was to mistreat him. He was just another person, trying best as he could to get through life despite all the people who wanted to make him miserable. And I learned a lot from him. It didn't take me long to be completely ashamed of my previous actions. Curtis was a gem. One of him was worth a thousand of the kids who gave him hell.

"So, anyway, I'm riding home on the bus one day, sitting next to Curtis, and this bully kid keeps shooting spit wads at him. Curtis was so used to being picked on that he didn't even react to it. But it pissed me off. I mean, who was this fucker? Picking on my friend right in front of me? Who the fuck did he think he was?

"I looked back at the kid. Told him to knock it the fuck off. He flipped me the bird. I pointed at him, said, 'You and me, Next stop.' So when the bus got to the next stop, I got off. The bully kid followed. And I proceeded to beat the ever-loving snot out of him, in front of everybody on the bus. Just righteously kicked his ass.

"Well, then I got in trouble with the school again. Sent to the principal's office again. I was sure I'd be in deep shit when dad got home that day. Turns out, I wasn't. The school called my folks again, the bus driver narced me out. I was suspended for fighting. Dad came to my room, told me to explain myself. So I told him what happened. I told him about the bully, and how I was standing up for my friend.

"My dad left the room. I thought he was going to get his belt or something. But when he came back, he had two bottles of Old Milwaukee in his left hand, and a church key in his right. He sat on the bed next to me, opened the beers, and handed me one. We clinked bottles, and that's when I had my first taste of beer. Dad said he was proud of me, that I had done the right thing, and that he hoped I'd kicked that other kid's ass good. Told me he'd handle the school, but that as far as he and mom were concerned, I was in no trouble at all.

"Dad can't keep me from being suspended, but he can keep it from feeling like a punishment. For the next week, I got to go on-base with my dad instead of going to school. I had friends bring me my schoolwork to do at home so I wouldn't fall behind. But the amazing thing was that all through that week I was suspended, other kids from the school were calling and asking me if they could sit next to Curtis while I was gone.

"Suddenly, it became the cool thing to do to stand up for the disadvantaged kids. Curtis went from being the school's dumping ground to something of an unofficial mascot. After my fight, anyone who picked on Curtis became the outcast. It just wasn't cool anymore, you know?. Anyway, it left me with a lasting distaste for the kind of people who think they can treat everyone like shit."

Vin looked at Terry for a moment after he'd finished his story. "OK," Vin said, tapping an ash in the ashtray on his desk. "I see why you're a writer now. You tell a good story. Now, write me a happy ending for this one." He reached into his inside pocket, pulled out an envelope, and handed it over to Terry. "Here's $2,500. Consider it an advance, to cover any expenses. I'll pay you another $2,500 when you turn the story in. Five grand, total." He paused for a beat. "And let me know if you want any muscle with you for anything. I can have that arranged."

"I'll do the best I can, Vin," Terry replied. Terry had never made that much money from a single story before. It was much more than he'd expected.

"One more thing," Terry said. "Can you put me in touch with the kid who was with your son when it happened?"

"I don't have a number or anything for him. All I know is his name is Dave Sims, or at least, that's what he told me when I met him in Brandon's hospital room."

"OK, that's probably enough. I'll see if the sheriff can track him down for me."

...

Vin followed Terry out as he left. He saw Terry unlock his Buick, and said, "Jesus, kid, is that piece of shit yours?" Terry nodded. "I'm not paying you enough." He looked the car up and down. "Tell you what, your rate just doubled." He reached into his pocket and pulled out a roll of bills. He counted off another $2,500 and handed it to Terry.

"Get a decent car, at least," Vin said as Terry took the offered wad of cash.

Terry knew that this wasn't an act of generosity. Vin was feeling him out, looking to see if maybe he had a place in Vin's pocket. The largesse was most likely a ploy meant to lure him in, Terry was sure. Still, he'd take the extra money. Who knew when he'd get work again?

17

The Dojo

After meeting with Vin Capriani, Terry thought about his next move as he eased his big Buick away from the curb. He wanted to talk to the witness, Dave Sims, but all he had was a name. Terry guessed that he still lived with his parents, and probably wouldn't be listed in the phone book. He knew there were ways of tracking him down, but figured the simplest would be to have the sheriff look him up. The sheriff might even want to send his own investigators out to talk to Sims.

Without much of a line on Sims yet, the obvious thing to do would be to go to Rincon Point beach and scope things out there. But he remembered Sheriff Baker's admonishment to not go alone. He also wanted to do a little preliminary work before going to see Rincon for himself.

So Terry did what he would have done as a reporter: He went to the beach in Ventura to interview surfers. He talked to a couple dozen people he found toting surfboards on San Buenaventura State Beach. He asked them whether they had ever surfed at Rincon Point, and if so, what their experiences were like.

A few didn't want to talk, which Terry brushed off. As a reporter, he knew some people didn't want to answer questions, especially when they're trying to have fun. Others were willing, but had nothing much to say. They hadn't surfed at Rincon. But half of the surfers he did talk to warned him not to go to Rincon. The general gist of their advice was that the surfers there were "real violent dickheads," and that trying to surf Rincon was "a good way to have a bad day."

Terry took down the names of the surfers who had something to say about Rincon, and made notes of their comments. He probably would not need them for anything, but he may decide to use them in the story, and if so, he'd want proper attribution for the quotes.

After spending an hour on the beach, Terry went back to his Buick and started driving. He pulled out the card the sheriff had given him at a stoplight and looked at the address. He knew where Front Street was. It was near the pier, which was on the beach he'd just left. He decided to go over there and check things out.

Eight Fifty-One East Front Street turned out to be a narrow storefront, barely wider than the door, with no signage other than "TAMBO Industries" painted on the glass of the front door. The storefront was mashed between an Italian deli and a shop that sold both bicycles and surfboards. It was conveniently located near the pedestrian bridge over the 101.

The door was locked, but there was a button for a buzzer, which Terry pushed. A few seconds later Terry heard footsteps and the door was opened by a stout fireplug of a man with tattooed arms. The man grinned at Terry.

"How may I help you?" the man asked.

"My name is Terry Cahill," Terry said. "Sheriff Baker referred me to you."

The door opened wider. "Come in," said the man with the tattoos. Terry walked through the doorway to find himself in a long hall leading toward the rear of the building. He followed his host back. The man with the tattoos led him to a large open space with pads, punching bags, and other training equipment visible. He turned and stuck out his hand.

"Lance Thompssen," he said. "I'm one of the owners of Ventura Pier Brazilian Jiu Jitsu. Welcome to our dojo." He gestured to the other three men in the room. "These are my partners, Brian Matthews, Marcel Washington, and Arturo Guzman."

"Nice to meet you all. Terry Cahill." Terry shook hands with each of the men. They were all impressively built. Terry found some satisfaction, though, in being the tallest man in the room. However, he figured any one of them could kick his ass. Call it a hunch.

"So, Tim said something about going to a beach with you?" Lance said.

"Uh, yeah," Terry said. "I'm looking into something for him, and he thought it might be good if I wasn't alone on this one."

"You look like you can handle yourself OK," Lance said. "Military?"

"Yeah, ex-Army," Terry replied. "Been out a few years now." Terry gave them a brief rundown of the story he was working on, and the Santa Barbara Boys surf gang he was expected to encounter should he snoop around Rincon Point.

"Sound like a bunch of dickheads," Brian said.

"Pretty much my thought too," agreed Terry. "I haven't come across any of them yet, but dickheads is my impression. I kinda want to just go over there and kick their asses."

"I'm down," Marcel said. The other three nodded in agreement.

"What say we grab our surfboards, gentlemen?" said Lance with a broad grin that looked like trouble. He looked at Terry. "Leave your car here and ride with us. We'll take the dojo van."

"Just like that?" Terry asked.

"Just motherfucking like that," Lance said, still grinning.

• • •

The five of them piled into an old Dodge van, one of those short ones from the '70s. It was lined inside with wood panels and shag carpeting, and had bubble windows and couch-like seating in the back. The surfboards were piled up against the right side where the sliding door was. The boards looked beat to hell, and Terry suspected that they were props.

They rode up PCH in that rattly van. The guys from the dojo were swapping jokes, funny stories, and laughing. Terry reverted back to his habit as a reporter and mostly sat back and observed the others on the drive north to Rincon. He was sitting in the back of the van with Lance.

"So, we're going up on a fact-finding mission, right?" Lance asked.

"Uh, yeah, basically," Terry said. "I just want to get the lay of the land, really, but if we can find someone to maybe ask a few questions, that might help."

"Yo, we're going to the same beach where those sharks attacked those people, aren't we?" Marcel asked from the passenger seat.

Terry was reminded of the articles he read about the surfers being bitten at Rincon Point, and wondered how that would affect his investigation. Maybe there wouldn't even be anyone there.

"Yeah, man," Brian chimed in. "I even brought barbecue sauce." The van erupted in laughter.

"Those poor fuckin' sharks," Lance said, shaking his head. "They'll never know what hit 'em."

•••

The drive up to the beach only took about 15 minutes, and Terry and Lance started talking. He asked Lance why the sheriff had sent him his way, and learned that the men he was traveling with trained deputies of the Ventura County Sheriff's Department in unarmed combat. The dojo had a contract with the county, and taught the police how to take down potentially violent subjects without severely injuring them, hopefully. Sheriff Baker was very conscious of things like lawsuits and public relations.

Once at their destination Brian made a u-turn on PCH and parked on the shoulder facing south. The guys grabbed their faded, battered surfboards and clambered down to the beach leaving one of their own, Marcel, behind to make sure nobody took their frustrations out on the group's van while they were there. Marcel casually leaned against the side of the van, pretending to inspect his fingernails.

They walked down to the stone-strewn beach carrying their faded old surfboards. The guys from the dojo let Terry borrow one of theirs. Terry didn't surf, and had no intention of going in the water. He still guessed it was more a prop than anything else, but wondered if any of the guys actually planned to surf.

There were four men hanging out at a stone pile on some relatively high ground on the thin strip of beach. They had surfboards too, but theirs looked a lot nicer than the ones Terry and his group were carrying. The men took notice. One of them said something.

"Uh-uh, no way, man," he shouted from his perch. "You don't want to go in there. No surfing today."

"Or ever!" said one of his friends.

"Looks fine to us," Arturo replied. Terry's group kept walking toward the shore.

The guys at the stone pile all stood up and started toward Terry and his companions.

"There's sharks in that water," one of them said.

"It's the ocean," Lance shot back. "Where else do you expect them to live?"

"There's land sharks, too, motherfucker," the surfer said as he attempted to shove Lance. But Lance had been braced for it, and the surfer who tried to push him ended up slipping and falling on his own ass.

Another surfer slapped the surfboard out of Brian's hands and it clattered on the rocky beach. Brian pointed down at his board and shouted "You fucked it up, you fucker." And then, much quicker than seemed possible, he buried an uppercut in the surfer's gut, knocking the wind out of him. The surfer fell over on his side, wheezing. Brian kicked him in the ribs while he was down, eliciting what would probably have been a scream of pain if he'd had any air in his lungs. It came out as a high-pitched moaning wheeze.

"You don't shut the fuck up, I'm gonna drag your ass into water for the sharks," Brian said to the man he'd just injured.

The third surfer had picked out Arturo, who grabbed his wrist when he tried to throw a punch, stepped inside it, and wrenched his arm up and behind him, and at the moment had his right arm twisted at an angle that didn't look possible.

The last surfer had singled out Terry, but seeing as how things were going for his friends at the moment, didn't seem particularly eager to attack. He reached down and picked up a handful of sand, and while he was bent over Terry swung the surfboard at him, catching him in the side with the edge of the board. He howled and went down, and Terry stepped on the back of his head, shoving his face into the coarse sand and holding it there.

Terry surveyed the situation and saw Lance on top of one of the surfers who looked like he'd been tied into a human pretzel. Arturo had taken the legs out from under his attacker and was still holding his wrist high behind his head. Brian was inspecting the chip in his surfboard and seemingly not paying any mind to the crumpled heap of surfer on the beach at his feet.

Brian walked over to the stone pile and began breaking the gang's surfboards in half. Lance and Chris saw this and cracked up with loud laughter.

"Looks like these land sharks don't have any teeth," Lance said, and they laughed harder.

"C'mom, man, let me up," Terry's attacker said. "I can't get any air." He coughed convincingly. Terry let up, reached down and grabbed the man's right arm, and roughly yanked him upright. The man started to cry out in pain, but then began coughing violently.

"Feel like talking?" Terry asked. "I've got some questions for you."

"I got a shitload of sand up my nose," the man said dejectedly.

"Good. I hope it's in your eyes, too. That is what you were planning to do to me, isn't it?"

"You're on our beach," the surfer said weakly.

"There are no private beaches in California," Terry replied. "They're all public. We have as much right to be here as anyone else. Now, somebody tries to throw sand in my face for being somewhere I have every right to be, I'm gonna kick his ass."

"What do you want?" the surfer asked.

"To start with, your name, and everybody else's name who's here."

Terry had a notebook and a pen with him, like he would had he been reporting, even though he did not expect an overwhelming amount of information. It took a little more convincing, but Terry was able to get a name from his assailant: Dewey Michaels. Michaels was apparently the one in charge of the Santa Barbara Boys. That, Terry thought, was probably the only useful piece of information he'd gotten from this trip.

But on the off chance that there might be something more, he took one of his old business cards from the paper out of his wallet and handed it to the surfer.

"You think of anything else you want to tell me, call that pager number and I'll get back to you," Terry said.

As Terry and the guys from the dojo were leaving, Scott Keener, the one he'd been talking to, said, "Man, you really fucked Billy up," looking over at the man whose ribs Brian had cracked. Billy indeed looked pretty bad, breathing in ragged gasps, the side of his body already starting to show what would be one hell of a bruise.

"I can't say I'm sympathetic," Terry replied. "You know you fuckheads put some kid in a coma? That asshole's gonna have a sore chest for a few months. Think he'd rather be in a hospital bed instead?"

Keener just looked at Terry sullenly.

"I didn't think so," Terry said.

• • •

When they got back to the van they found Marcel playing with a butterfly knife, flipping and twirling the blade around its handles. "Hey guys," he said. "Look at what I got."

"Ooh, that is nice," Lance said. "Where could you have possibly found that?"

"One of those surf-gang guys was kind enough to try and pop our tires with it," he said. "I didn't let him."

"You know those things are illegal, right?" Lance asked.

"Guess I won't show it to Sheriff Tim, then," Marcel said, flipping the knife closed and putting it in his pocket.

They piled back into the van with their surfboards a little worse for the wear than when they had gotten there. None of them had gone surfing.

18

First Report

It was mid afternoon when the van pulled back in behind the dojo on Front Street. As he was saying his goodbyes, Lance shook his hand again.
"Hey, you should come train with us," Lance said.
"Really?" Terry asked. "I've never thought about it before today, but that stuff you guys did? Man, yeah, I wouldn't mind picking up some of those moves."
"It's not just about the moves, man. It's a whole way of life."
"Like surfing?"
"Ha! Yeah, like they say about surfing anyway."
"Well, thank you," Terry said. "I'll take you up on that. When do you guys train?"
"All the time, or as much as we can. Some of us have day jobs. I work in finance, actually. But there's usually someone here. I'll introduce you around to the members you haven't met yet."
Terry handed Lance another of his business cards from his old job, and told him the pager number on it was still good.
"Speaking of," Lance said, holding up the card, "I'm not so sure you should have given that guy one of these. Now he knows who you are."
Terry hadn't considered that, but thought about it for a moment. He felt he had handed his card out to more dangerous people than Keener.

"All he's really got there is a name and a pager number," Terry said. "I don't work at the paper anymore. I don't think there's anything he can do to me but blow up my pager."

"Maybe," Lance said. He didn't ask why Cahill's life seemed to be starting over from scratch, even though he was curious. "Still, watch your back for the next few days. You never know."

"Thanks," Terry said as they parted ways.

It was long past lunchtime, and Terry realized he hadn't eaten anything yet that day. He was starving. He saw Delissi's Italian Deli as he was headed back to his Buick, and changed direction. He ordered a large Italian sub with a bag of salt and vinegar chips and a can of Schaefer. It was delicious. Life was pretty good.

Terry found it somewhat troubling that he wasn't more bothered by the violence that had transpired just more than an hour ago on the beach. He wondered if it was because the people who'd gotten beaten up had done worse to a lot of other people. But part of him worried that it was more because he was just emotionally deadened since the day he caught his wife cheating. He wondered if he'd ever be the same again, or if the numbness was permanent.

He had a shift that evening bartending at the Beam Reach, so when he was done with his meal he decided to go back to the marina, rinse off the salt and sand from the beach, and change into some fresh clothes. The big Buick fired up obediently and wafted him back to his temporary home in air-conditioned comfort.

Though Terry didn't have a phone living on *Easy Goer*, he was glad to still have his pager. The newspaper had refused to pay for them, so all the reporters who had one, and almost all of them did, payed for them personally. Terry's pager went off as he was changing into clean clothes, having just returned from the shower. He recognized the number in the display as Sheriff Baker's direct line, finished getting ready, and headed over to the Reach a little early so he could call in.

"Heard there was a bit of a dust-up at Rincon today," Tim started.

"Yeah," Terry replied. "Santa Barbara Boys, up to their usual it seems."

"I could use a beer. I'm gonna swing by the Reach when I get out of here. I'd like to go over it with you. You be there?"

"Yeah, I'm on-shift tonight."

"See you in a little while," the sheriff said.

"Oh, hey, sheriff?"

"Yeah?"

"Before I forget, I wanted to ask you if you can track someone down for me. That kid who was with Brandon Capriani at Rincon. His name is Dave Sims. I want to talk to him. Can you get an address for me?"

"Shouldn't be a problem."

"Thanks, sheriff."

• • •

Terry was behind the bar when Sheriff Baker came in. He reached into the beer bin behind him and popped a Dos Equis for his friend, stuffed a lime wedge in the bottle's mouth, and slid it over.

"Thank you," Tim said, taking a swig. He handed Terry a slip of paper with an address on it. "That's Sims's address, at least according to the DMV."

"Thanks."

"So, tell me how it went down today. I'm not exactly happy that you guys went up there and kicked a bunch of ass. We're trying to get information here, not provoke these guys."

"I know," Terry said. "But I didn't expect to get any useful information by asking these clowns a bunch of questions. I wanted to see if their reaction to people surfing at that beach was as extreme as it had been made out to be, or if it was a bunch of bullshit." He paused, looking his friend in the eye. "It wasn't bullshit."

"Lance said they came at you pretty hard."

"They were more aggressive than competent," Terry said. A pretty young woman at the bar signaled him for another drink, and he excused himself to go take care of her. When he got back, he started again. "Where was I? Oh, yeah, so they were willing to fight and fight dirty. I don't think they were too worried about the consequences of committing an assault in public in broad daylight. Pretty brazen, really. Makes me wonder."

"You think they're protected?"

"Maybe. Maybe they just don't care. Or maybe they've been getting away with it for so long that they've gotten complacent."

"But only one of those possibilities escalates the severity of what we're looking at here," Tim said.

"Yeah, exactly. If they don't care, they'll probably be easier to bust. Same if they're just too comfortable with what they're doing. But if they're protected, that means we can't count on any kind of cooperation from Santa Barbara, and ..."

"Vin might go to war," Tim said, finishing Terry's unspoken thought.

"And that would be bad."

"Thank you, Captain Understatement." He finished his beer and Terry slid a fresh one over to him without being asked. "Well, OK, but this is the last one, thanks. Gotta make it home for dinner with the Missus. So, what's your next move gonna be?"

"I played a hunch at the beach. I think I may have a potential source. The surfer who attacked me, well, tried to attack me, seemed like the weakest of the few I met. I gave him my card and told him to page me if he wanted to talk about anything. Something tells me I might hear from him. Until then, I've got a name I want to look into."

"You won't be bringing Lance et al. to brace him, will you?" Tim asked.

"No, strictly research. I'll be in the library."

"Good. What's the name?"

"Dewey Michaels."

"Look up Alton, too."

"Who's he?" Terry asked.

"Dewey's dickhead father."

19

Uncomfortable Conversation

Santa Barbara Sheriff's Department Deputy Kerry Kirkham was sitting in a reception area outside Dewey Michaels's office. It was spacious and the furniture plush, but being kept waiting got on Kirkham's nerves. So did being summoned by Dewey like some kind of servant.

Dewey's secretary motioned to the deputy and told him he could go in now, and Kirkham tossed the issue of *Life* magazine he was reading onto the coffee table in front of him, stood up, and walked to the tall double doors that led into Dewey's office. Dewey stood up as Kirkham walked in, and came around his desk to shake hands.

More glad-handing bullshit, Kirkham thought with an inner sigh of resignation. He dealt with politicians regularly enough in his job to recognize the type, and bankers, he found, were often cut from the same cloth, only worse.

"Good afternoon, Dewey," Kirkham said, shaking the other man's hand.

"Good to see you," Dewey Michaels said, with too much enthusiasm to really mean it. "How's your dad these days?"

"He's good. Hates retirement, but what are you gonna do?" Kirkham shrugged. He deliberately didn't ask how Dewey's family was doing. He didn't want to stand around here bullshitting all afternoon before getting to business. He'd been asked here for a reason, and he wanted to get down to it.

Michaels sat back behind his desk and Kirkham took a seat on the other side. He waited for Michaels to start the real conversation.

"So, two of us gone, huh?" Michaels opened.

"Yeah. Fuckin' sharks, man. Can you believe that shit?"

"No, Kerry. I can't believe it. I've been surfing all my life. I've never even seen a fucking shark near the shore. Now two of us have been killed by them? I find that difficult to swallow."

"Well, for what it's worth, you're not the only one."

"What do you mean by that?"

"Dicker is looking into Jon-Jon like it might be a homicide is what I mean by it."

'Dicker' is what some of the deputies called Rick Decker. He hated the nickname 'Dick,' not so much for its phallic connotations as for the alliteration with his last name. He felt it made him sound like a made-up character. Of course, hating it just made something worse stick.

"You mean like someone made the shark bite him? How would that ..."

"No, Dewey. Jon-Jon died in the hospital. Dicker has been sniffing around there, from what I hear. Nothing official yet, as far as I know, but if he didn't think something was there he'd have dropped it by now."

"Shit, does that mean Jon-Jon's house has been searched by the cops?"

"I'd bet on it, yes. Routine." Kirkham almost enjoyed making Michaels squirm.

"You don't think there's anything there for them to find, do you?"

"No telling Jon-Jon was a slob. Chances are even if something is there it's buried under crap. I don't think we have anything to worry about."

Michaels thought about that for a moment. "Man, who'd want to kill Jon-Jon?"

"Not my department," Kirkham said. *Are you kidding me?* he thought. *Jon-Jon was a goddamn prick. Probably lots of people out there wanted to kill him.*

"You seem awfully unconcerned by this all."

"Like I said before, I don't think we've got anything to worry about. Just because Dicker thinks Jon-Jon was murdered doesn't mean he was. And even if he was, whoever did it probably did us a favor."

"Jon-Jon was my best friend since childhood," Michaels said quietly. "That's not what I'd call a favor."

"Jon-Jon was a liability, and now he's gone. I know you were friends, but the truth is he was gonna get us all fried someday. He was out of control, and you know it. It's why you're worried about there being something to find now that he's gone. It's better this way. We don't have to cover for him anymore, which is a good thing. Keeping him out of jail was gonna land us in jail eventually."

"And what about Shane?"

"Shane was killed by a big-ass shark. I was there, man. I saw the whole thing. No human involvement. Just a fuckin' great white that decided to see what he tasted like and bit the guts right out of him."

"You think the shark did us a favor there?"

"No, I liked Shane."

"I did too. Can you snoop around Decker's case on Jon-Jon, see what's happening with it?"

"A little bit. Gotta be careful, 'cause he won't like it if he finds out I'm fucking with his case. But some curiosity is expected here, and cops like to gossip just like anyone else. I'll see what I can pick up hanging around the station. Best I can promise."

"OK, do it."

And with that, Kirkham knew he'd been dismissed.

20

Meeting is Called

Billy Newhouse was not happy. He'd been checked out at St. Francis for the injuries he'd sustained on the beach earlier that day. The good news was that he was not badly injured. The bad news was that he had four cracked ribs, and they hurt like a motherfucker. His entire left side was one big purple bruise. And there wasn't much of anything the docs could do about any of it.

He had called a meeting of the Santa Barbara Boys at his house. There were seven of them there, not the whole gang, but not everyone was available. In addition to the five men who had been at Rincon that day, there was Kerry Kirkham and Pete Edwards. The men from the incident on the beach were telling the others an exaggerated version of what had happened.

"They broke all our fucking surfboards in half," Jeremy Dodd was saying. "They came onto our beach, they started a fight, they vandalized our property. We can't let that go, man. We gotta go after these guys and show them they can't fuck with us like that."

"Who the fuck do you think you're kidding?" Kirkham said.

"What the fuck do you mean?" Dodd responded.

"I mean, we've been the ones starting fights on that beach for a couple of decades now, and I'm damned sure you guys started this one. Only difference is, this time you got your asses handed to you."

"Them coming to our beach was them starting the fight," Dodd said, but some of the wind had been taken out of his sails.

"Look, I don't like outsiders stealing our waves any more than you do. But don't give me that shit about 'they started it.' We've always started it. It's our fucking beach, and we got a right. But you assholes better learn how to handle yourselves if you're gonna defend our territory."

"I got their plates when I went up there to pop their tires," Don Harris offered. "You could put it in the computer, we could track them down and go fuck them up." Harris was absent-mindedly scratching the 9-inch long cut on his leg from the shark attack. The stitches itched.

"Let me think on that a bit," Kirkham said. "If they're local, it might be better to ask them to join us. Hell, we could use guys who can fight like that on our side. But I do want to know who they are."

"License plate said 'TAMBO' on it," Harris said. He spelled it out for Kirkham. "And they ain't local. I've never seen them around here before."

"Keener got one of their cards," Billy Newhouse offered. "We got one of their names."

"And why did he give you that?" Harris asked with a tone of accusation in his voice.

"Let up on Keener," Kirkham warned. Then to Keener, "Let me see that card, though."

21

Again

The killer was on his victim's doorstep. It was dark outside. Not exactly the dead of night, but late enough that people would be inside, watching their TVs and getting ready for bed. He had parked two blocks away and walked here, and hoped that wouldn't be noticed. Otherwise, he was confident that he would get away with it again. He knocked on the door, which was opened a few seconds later.

"Oh, hey," the victim said. "Come on in." He was a night owl, and visitors in the late hours were not unusual for him.

"Thanks," the killer said, stepping inside.

"You want a beer?"

"Sure, that sounds good," the killer said. His victim went over to the fridge and got out two bottles of Sierra Nevada pale. He uncapped them and handed one to the man who would end his life.

"So what brings you here tonight?" the victim asked. He took a swig of beer. "This isn't about that beach shit, is it?"

"Nah. Thought I'd come by and check out that new Edelbrock manifold you got on the Camaro. Been thinking of upgrading, myself. Wanted to see what you thought of it now that you've got it on there."

"Sure, we can go take a look. You think it'll fit on your Nova?"

"That's one of the things I wanted to see. It should, long as it's not too tall." The killer took a big pull off his own bottle of beer.

"Well, let me get my keys," the victim said. "We can go out to the garage and you can check it out."

The killer smiled to himself.

"So, you really think you'll pull the trigger this time?" the victim asked.

"Something like that," the killer said. He was following his victim out to the garage, who didn't see the smirk that accompanied the statement. He pulled the pair of latex gloves out of the pocket of his jacket and slipped them onto his hands.

As the killer followed him into the garage, he shot his foot out in front of his victim's leg and hooked it while grabbing a handful of his hair at the back of his head. He took the victim's legs out from under him and slammed his forehead directly into edge of the front fender of the old Camaro as he went down.

The victim slumped down to the pavement in front of the car with a groan. His killer took the car keys out of his hand and opened the driver's side door of the Camaro. He put the key in the ignition and started the engine. It came to life and settled into a loping idle. The killer shut the car's door, and exited the house through the back door.

Shouldn't take long, the killer thought. *No pollution controls on that baby.*

He picked up his beer and walked down the street, disappearing into the night.

22

Listening

It was late, or early, depending on one's perspective, when Terry got home to *Easy Goer* and settled in for what he hoped would be a decent night's sleep. He was lying in the bow berth listening to the sound of the water lapping at the hull and trying to relax enough to drift off to sleep when he heard it.

It was the sound of the marina's dock cart rolling again.

He was curious, so he got up and carefully went up on deck to see if he could catch a glimpse of whomever was loading up a boat with something at this time of night. Or morning, depending on one's perspective.

He was in some luck. There was enough moonlight to see fairly well, but by the time he was outside the person using the cart had already passed by and was obscured by the boat next to him. He stayed crouched there in *Easy Goer's* cockpit, keeping his head down, but watching. Listening. He could hear the sound of something heavy being handled, footsteps that landed a bit too heavily.

A breeze picked up and blew a gagging stench right at Terry. It hit him like a fist, and he almost threw up. He calmed his stomach at the last second and regained some of his composure. It was just enough to prevent him from vomiting.

What in the unholy fuck is that? he wondered.

The person who had been using the cart did not bring it back to its area on shore. Instead, Terry heard the sound of a boat being pushed out of its slip. But he didn't hear an engine start. Just the sound of a hull moving through water nearby. He caught a shadow on the water, but it didn't tell him much.

He waited a couple of minutes, but heard nothing other than the usual marina sounds when people weren't around. When he was sure the boat was gone, he hopped off *Easy Goer* and walked down the dock toward where he thought the sound was coming from. There was an empty slip three slips down from where *Easy Goer* was moored. On the finger where the boat's port side would face sat the now-empty dock cart.

Terry made a mental note of which slip it was. He wasn't sure why, but he wanted to see what kind of boat was going out at such a time.

•••

The night was bittersweet in a way for Dave Sims. His final run out to the coast just off Rincon Point would be happening soon. He would have been happy to continue the outings, inspired by the stack of unused lobster cages he'd found in a barn on his family's property out near Somis. He'd even gotten to the point where the stink of rotting meat didn't immediately make him vomit, just gave him an uneasy stomach.

But he had almost run out of lobster cages. After these he'd be down to the last two. He didn't think they'd be missed.

23

Studying

The next morning found Terry awake earlier than he had hoped. He'd only gotten about five hours of sleep, but this time it was a deep sleep. Probably the best he'd had since this whole thing had started. He got up, put on his robe, and went out onto *Easy Goer's* cockpit with a mug of hot tea to enjoy the morning before getting his day started.

The gray and white cat he'd been talking to walked down the dock.

"Hi, Kitty," Terry said. The cat paused behind *Easy Goer* and regarded Terry.

"Mrow."

"Yeah, me too, man," Terry said to the cat. The cat looked as if he were making up his mind about something, then casually hopped up onto *Easy Goer's* fantail and into the cockpit. He walked around a bit, sniffing here and there, checking things out and nonchalantly pretending to ignore Terry. Terry just kept drinking his tea and let the cat look around. Eventually he hopped up on the seat opposite Terry, sat down, and started bathing.

Terry didn't move or say anything. He just kind of enjoyed the moment. He didn't even hear Wendy approaching.

"Looks like you've made friends with Charlie," Wendy said.

"Oh, hey, hi, Wendy. Come aboard, please."

"Thank you," she said, ascending the dock stairs. She crossed over to the other side of the cockpit and sat next to the cat, who bumped his head against her knee. She gave him a scratch on the top of his head, which he seemed to like.

"So that's his name? Charlie?"

"Yeah, he's our dock cat," she said.

"Oh, he belongs to the marina?"

"No, he lives here. Might have been a stray, might have been someone's pet who got lost while his people were docked. But he sticks around here, and some of the people who live or work here kinda look out for him. He's bunked with me on *Clara* a few times."

"Well," Terry said, looking over at the cat. "It's nice to meet you, Charlie."

"Mrow," Charlie said. He looked content.

"Hey, do you happen to know who has the slip three down from *Easy Goer?*"

"Not offhand, but I could find out. Why?"

"It's probably nothing. I've just heard them leaving a couple of times at like 3 a.m. now, and I'm curious."

"That is kind of an odd hour," Wendy said. "I'll see if I can get the harbormaster to tell me who's there. It could be someone taking joyrides or something."

"Thanks."

"You got plans today?" Wendy asked.

"Yeah, going to drive out to Somis, see if I can talk to somebody. Then off to the library to do a little research. I'm sort of looking into something for Tim. What's your day look like?"

"No charters today, so I'll be at the Reach. I might get behind the bar today. It's been a little while, and it's more fun than paying bills and balancing the books."

Terry chatted with Wendy for a little while longer before she went on her way. Charlie the cat stayed on the seat, looking relaxed and resuming his bath.

• • •

Before getting into his day, Terry decided it would probably be a good idea to check in with Vin. He didn't have much to report, but he didn't want his client to think he was ducking him. He used the payphone outside the Beam Reach to call in.

"You got something already?" Vin asked.

"Not much yet. I went up to Rincon with a few friends to scout the place out. We were not welcomed warmly. Four surfer goons tried to kick our asses, another one tried to slash our tires."

"Tried?"

"We didn't let them," Terry said simply. "We ended up kicking their asses instead."

Vin responded with a hearty laugh. "I thought you didn't want to use any muscle on this."

"It was more like protection. You know, just in case. Like a condom in your wallet. Anyway, I didn't get much more than a few names and the lay of the land, but I'm going to look into some people and see what I find. I'll let you know if I get anything good."

"You're not going to tell me the names?"

"Not right now, no. Could be bullshit. Let me look into them some. If there's something to them, I'll definitely keep you informed. But I wouldn't put it past these bozos to make some shit up, maybe even feed me the names of their own enemies or something like that."

"All right, kid. You handle it your way. For now."

"Thanks, Vin. Like I said, I'll keep you informed."

• • •

It was still relatively early when Terry walked out to the parking lot and hopped in his Buick. The marine layer had yet to burn off, and the morning was cool with damp air. Terry had a lightweight windbreaker on over a plain t-shirt and jeans, and was wearing the sneakers he'd recently bought at Kmart.

As usual, the Buick fired up right away, and Terry let it warm up a bit so he could run the heater for the drive. He got on the 101 South and took it to where the 126 split off. The morning rush had mostly subsided by then, but Terry knew that there were spots in Oxnard and Camarillo where the 101 slowed down for no discernible reason, so he decided to go the back way, taking the 126 and then exiting at Wells Road near Saticoy. He followed Wells until it ended at the old 118, then took a left.

The drive took him through farming country, the two lane ribbon of old 118 cutting through fields of citrus groves, strawberry patches, and the occasional stand of avocado trees, with tall eucalyptus trees serving as both windbreaks and markers of property lines. He cracked the driver's side window and took in the fresh air, scented with citrus blossoms and eucalyptus and pepper trees. It was a smell he associated with California.

Sims's address was on Old Balcolm Canyon Road in Somis, a small farming community where the citrus groves were becoming dotted with the large new houses of well-off growers and people who wanted to escape city life, but not be too far away from it. It was next-door to the suburb of Camarillo. Sims lived in one of those houses, confirming Terry's suspicion that he lived with his folks.

The house was large, with a circular driveway behind an iron gate, and tucked away between two large orange groves. The property was shaded by several pepper trees, and it appeared that there were a couple of out buildings in addition to the house. Terry assumed that the house had been built sometime within the last three years.

There was an intercom box mounted near the gate, and Terry pulled up to it and pushed the button. He waited several seconds before getting an answer.

"Yeah?" a voice squawked from the box.

"Mr. David Sims?" Terry asked. He thought at this hour Dave's parents would probably be at work.

"Uh, yeah," The voice said. "What is it?"

"My name is Terry Cahill. I'm a friend of Vin Capriani. I was wondering if you could talk to me about what happened on the beach a few days ago. Do you have a couple of minutes?"

"Uh, yeah, I guess so."

The gate began to open, and Terry drove through, parking on the circular drive. As he was getting out of his car, he saw one of the doors of the three-car garage opening. There was a silver Saab 900 Turbo parked inside. A physically fit looking young man came out as door reached the top of its travel. He had a fading shiner on his left eye.

"Jesus, I hope that thing doesn't leak oil," Sims said, pointing at the Electra. "My parents will kill me if it leaves spots on the driveway. You really know Vin Capriani?

"Yeah, he's the one who asked me to talk to you." Terry reached out to shake Sims's hand, which was met with a lack of enthusiasm.

"Well, I don't know what I can tell you, other than Brandon and I got beat up at the beach by some fucking Nazis, and Brandon's all fucked up because of it."

"If you would, just walk me through the incident. Tell me as much as you remember. What time did you get there?" Terry pulled a notebook and pen from the inside pocket of his windbreaker.

"Around noon, I guess," Sims said. "The June Gloom was mostly burned off and the wind was starting to pick up. We wanted to get there when there were some waves, y'know."

"How many people were there?"

"Besides me and Brandon? Just the five guys who came to kick our asses."

"Can you describe them?"

"They looked like surfers, man. What do you expect?"

"Were they tall, or short? Hair color? Eye color? Any tattoos or identifying marks?"

"They were mostly average surfers, y'know. Average height, all had tans, all seemed to be in shape, nobody was fat or anything. But the guy who knocked Brandon down, I do remember that fucker. He was big. Hairy, too. Like a damn ape."

"Dark hair, light hair?"

"Dark, man. Like an ape."

"How tall?"

"Maybe a couple inches taller than you. I dunno, it's hard to say. It's not like I brought a tape measure. But he was taller than me, and I think probably taller than you too."

"And big?"

"Yeah, big. Not fat, not a body builder, just big, man. He seemed to be leading the thing. The others kinda followed him."

"Do you remember anything about the others?"

"Not really. They were kicking my ass. I didn't take notes."

"OK, what happened after they approached you?"

"They beat the shit out of us, man! What do you think? They gave me a black eye and a fat lip, bruised me up good, fucked up my ribs. Then all of a sudden it stopped. I looked around, they were gone. Then I saw Brandon lying there on the rocks with blood pouring out of his head."

"What did you do then?"

"First? I panicked. I thought he was dead. I didn't know what to do, I was just kinda frozen there, y'know. Then I saw him move, and I kinda snapped out of it. I knew I needed to get him help. I ran across the street and found a call box on PCH. I called for help, then went back to

Brandon and waited for the ambulance to get there. That's it, man. That's everything that happened."

"OK, thanks. I think that helps." Terry wrote his pager number on a page of the notebook, then tore it off and handed it to Sims. "That's my pager number. If you think of anything, I'd appreciate it if you'd give me a call."

"Sure," Sims said, with even less enthusiasm than his handshake.

Terry got back in his Buick and Sims went back in his parents' house.

It was nearing lunchtime, and Terry's stomach made its emptiness known. This worked out well, timing wise, with what he needed to do next. He took a detour to Lewis Road and stopped at the Somis Market to use the payphone. He needed to call Herb.

Herb Easton ran the *VC Monitor's* morgue, where the newspaper kept its archives. He could look up articles on microfiche at the library, but he needed to know which articles to look up, which papers to find them in and the dates they were printed. The library would have the papers, but no way of searching for the specific names he was looking for.

But the *Monitor* had access to ProQuest, a computerized searchable database that could take keywords and find articles with those words, or in this case, names, present. The big central library in downtown Los Angeles also had ProQuest, but it was a considerable drive getting there and back. Terry figured he could save himself a hell of a lot of time, frustration, and gasoline by persuading Herb to look up the stories for him. Besides, Herb was much more experienced with these kind of searches than Terry was. What would take him hours would take Herb something like 15 minutes, he was sure.

Of course, being *persona non grata* at the *Monitor* complicated matters somewhat. He couldn't just walk right in there like the old days and ask for what he wanted. But he and Herb had always been on friendly terms, Herb having been an Army veteran himself who had served on the same base in Germany Terry had, only two decades previous to Terry's service.

And Herb was a sucker for a free lunch. Which was fortunate, because Terry couldn't afford a more extravagant form of bribery. He walked over to the payphone outside the green-painted little stucco building of the market and dialed Herb's extension by memory.

"Hey, Cahill," Herb said. "Didn't expect to hear from you. I heard Marty fired your ass." This was what Herb considered a greeting.

"Yeah, Herb. He said he couldn't trust a vet to cover the cops."

"That prick. So what do you want, Cahill?"

"I was hoping you could help me find some articles. I've got some stuff I need run down on ProQuest, and I don't have access anymore." Terry pulled his notebook out and flipped to the notes he'd taken at the library.

"What are the keywords?" Herb asked.

"Bunch of names, actually." He read a list of names to Herb, starting with Dewey and Alton Michaels. "It's in connection with a violent surf gang up in Santa Barbara." Then, on a whim, he added, "And if you could, pull up some stories going back as far as you can on the history of shark attacks at the local beaches, say, from Silver Strand to Rincon?"

"So, what's in it for me? I got a job to do, y'know, and you don't work here anymore."

Terry could tell he may have asked for a bit too much with that last request.

"You know Delissi's Italian Deli, on Front Street?"

"Best Italian subs in Ventura," Herb said. "Yeah, I know 'em."

"Meet me there for lunch and I'll buy you a sub and a beer. That work?"

"That works. I'll see you there."

Terry hung up the payphone, got back in his Buick, and aimed it toward Ventura.

Terry got to Delissi's a few minutes ahead of his friend from the newspaper, and didn't wait to order. He picked a cold roast beef and provolone on a soft roll, heavy mayo, light mustard, and no onions or tomatoes. Herb walked in as the sandwich was being built, and ordered himself a large Italian with all the fixings. They each got a can of Schaefer and a bag of chips to round out their meals.

"I got a couple of lists for you," Herb said, handing over a computer printout with one hand while admiring the huge sub he was holding in the other, dripping Italian dressing onto the butcher paper below. Terry slid the printout over to his side of the table before unwrapping his own sandwich. It was fairly thick. Either Herb was thorough, or there was a lot out there about the Santa Barbara Boys and shark attacks.

"Much appreciated, Herb."

"Anytime, for a fellow vet. You got dicked over by Marty." He took an ambitious bite of the sub.

"Yeah, well, I probably wouldn't be the first or the last in that line. I appreciate it all the same, Herb."

"Hey, you want to buy me a Delissi's sub, you can feel free to hit me up once a week as far as I'm concerned. Hell, make it twice a week."

"I'll keep that in mind."

• • •

The E.P Foster library was on Main Street downtown, just across the 101 and a bit west of the Marina. Terry took California Street over from Delissi's. He hooked a right on Main and found street parking not too far from the library.

The library was a largish white building in a style common to mid-century construction, built in 1958. He knew where to find what he wanted there. Terry had been using the library for research for the last few years as a reporter, and was familiar with how to use the microfiche readers. He checked the printout Herb had given him, then went over to the microfiche, pulled the slides he wanted and took them over to a microfiche reader.

Most of the stories about Dewey Michaels were published in the business section of newspapers or in professional journals, and centered on his role as vice president of Margate Bank, a small regional chain of banks that existed primarily in California's Central Coast area, with its headquarters in Santa Barbara. Alton Michaels was the owner and chief executive of the chain, a position he had inherited.

The business articles turned out to be nothing particularly interesting. There were a couple of lawsuits here and there, but they appeared to have all been either settled out of court, or decided favorably for the bank. But Herb had also cross indexed their names with the words "surfing," "surfer" and "surf." Those searches only produced a couple of results, but they were much more interesting.

The first article Terry read was a profile of a local Santa Barbara surfing club dating back to January 1979. The surfing club, known then as just "The Boys," got a few column inches in a Santa Barbara paper basically about crazy kids who were so dedicated to surfing they were on the beach year-round. There was a single picture of six young men standing on the beach with their surfboards stuck tail-first in the sand next to them. The photo was captioned with their names and noted the location as Rincon Point beach.

Terry wrote the names in his notebook, along with the page number and date of the article and the name of the paper that published it. The names were Dewey Michaels, Jonathan Abernathy, Bradley Keane, William Newhouse, Peter Edwards, and Shane Larson.

The next article Terry read went all the way back to July 1959. It was a story published by the *LA Times* regarding a trend among a growing subset of surfers who were wearing Nazi paraphernalia and scaring off beachgoers with aggressive acts. These surf Nazis could be found on beaches up and down the Southern California coast, including at Rincon Point, where one of the people interviewed was listed as Alton Michaels. He was one of the Nazis.

So, that's interesting, Terry thought. *Like father, like son?* He wrote down the info for this story too, then considered and went back to the microfiche index to look up the Santa Barbara and Ventura County papers from around the same time to see if similar stories were published in the area. He came up dry. *Alton Michaels was one of the original surf Nazis, but it doesn't seem to have hurt his career and it looks like the only story linking him to that was published about 60 miles away from Santa Barbara. And that was 32 years ago.*

He made a few more notes and was getting ready to leave the library when he felt his pager vibrate. He pulled it off his belt and looked at the display. He didn't know the number, but he recognized the phone exchange as being from Carpinteria, just south of Santa Barbara. Terry knew that there was a payphone outside, across Main from the library. He headed over there and pulled some quarters from his pocket.

The other end of the line was answered by a man obviously trying to disguise his voice. "This Cahill?" the voice rasped.

"Yes, Terry Cahill," Terry said. "I got a page from this number."

"Listen, I don't have long," the man said. "They killed him, man."

"They killed whom?" Terry asked, now on alert. The call could be fake, but something about the urgency in the stranger's voice suggested otherwise.

"Man, don't you even read your own paper? Keener. They killed him. And I don't want to be next, so I shouldn't even be talking to you, y'dig?"

"Uh, yeah, I don't really work there any lo— ..."

"Whatever, man. They killed him for talking to you, on the beach that day."

"You sure about that?" Terry asked, alarmed again. "He didn't really tell me much of anything. How can you be sure this 'they' killed him? Are you talking about the Santa Barbara Boys?"

"Look, man, this thing goes back farther than you know. Like, way back."

"How far?" Terry asked. "You're not giving me much to go on."

"August 8, 1984. They killed her, too, man. They killed her and got away with it. Jon-Jon did it, now he's dead too. It goes back to there. There was some stuff before that, but you get to that and you'll have them."

The sound of the line going dead cut off Terry's next question. He held the phone out for a few seconds before hanging it back up. He walked back across the street and went back inside the library, going straight to the periodicals section where he found a copy of that day's *VC Monitor*.

He was sidetracked from looking up Keener by the *Monitor's* page-one story above the fold. He'd been reading the *Times* instead, mostly out of spite, and had missed seeing the local paper's coverage of recent events. The story was about the recent shark attacks at Rincon. Terry scanned the story, which was covered in fairly gory detail. There was a sidebar about how both of the attacks had proven fatal, as a surfer named Jonathan Abernathy who had lost his leg in the first attack later succumbed in St. Francis hospital.

Terry recognized the name. He pulled out his notebook and found the list of names from one of the stories about the surf gang, and noted that two of the men listed, Abernathy and Larson, were dead from the shark attacks.

He flipped through the News section until finding the story about a man named Scott Keener who had been found dead of an apparent suicide in his garage. Even though he remembered the name, he was still shocked to see the image of Keener and have it confirmed: He was the surfer Terry had given his business card to the day before on Rincon. The story implied that Keener had started his car in the garage with the door shut, then exited the car and stood next to it until the fumes overcame him.

That's odd, Terry thought. *I'd think most people killing themselves that way would stay sitting in the car. But Keener was found on the ground next to his car.* It didn't read right to Terry.

He went back to the microfiche slides and pulled the *LA Times* for dates ranging between August 8, 1984, and the end of the month. It took some searching, but he found an obituary in the August 11, 1984 edition about a women's surfing champion named Danielle Winfield who had drowned while surfing Rincon Point beach on August 8.

"They killed her, too, man," Terry heard the stranger say in his head, and a chill ran all the way down him.

Terry put the microfiche slides away and left the library. He had spent most of the afternoon there. He checked his watch and decided to go straight to the sheriff's office to share what he'd learned with Tim.

He pointed his Buick east and drove toward the sheriff's office on South Victoria Street on the other side of town. Traffic was thickening up due to the rush hour, and he hoped he would get there before Tim left. He hadn't wanted to take the time to call first.

The Ventura County Government Complex was a sprawling, for Ventura, collection of sand-colored concrete buildings that housed the county courthouses and most government offices, including the sheriff's. It had been built in the late '70s, and already looked dated with its polished floors of red brick and amber-stained wooden interior doors. When he got to the main entrance he caught Sheriff Baker just as he was walking out the door.

"Hey, Terry," Baker said. "What's up?"

"I might have something on these surf guys," Terry said. "Can we go back up to your office and talk about it?"

"I'd kinda prefer to keep this out of the office," Tim said. "But you're already here, and there aren't that many people in the office now. I guess it would be all right."

Once in the sheriff's personal office, Terry began relating what he'd learned over the day, starting with the things he'd discovered about Dewey and Alton Michaels.

"It's interesting, but it's not exactly a smoking gun, Terry," Tim said.

"I'm getting to that," Terry said, explaining the phone call to the stranger in Carpinteria.

"How do you know the call came from Carpinteria?" Tim asked.

"It was a 684 exchange. As far as I know that only covers Carp."

"Let's see if we can narrow it down further. This caller is someone I'd like to talk to. We need to see if we can find out who he is."

Tim flipped through his Rolodex, found the card he wanted, and picked up the handset of the phone on his desk and dialed out. "Hi, Mabel, it's Sheriff Baker" he said. "Listen, I need you to look up a number in the reverse directory for me." Terry handed over his pager, and Tim read the number off the display. He put his hand over the mouthpiece and looked at Terry "What time did you get this page?" he asked. Terry's Motorola Bravo pager displayed only a phone number with no time stamp.

"Just after 3 o'clock," Terry said. "Call it 3:05, maybe 3:10."

"Yeah, Mabel, can you trace down the address for one number, and then trace any calls made out to this other number right around 3 o'clock?" He gave Mabel Terry's pager number. "It's OK, the owner of the number is sitting right here. He authorizes it, I don't need a warrant."

"Hi, Mabel," Terry said, even though he was pretty sure she wouldn't hear it.

"OK, thanks," he said, writing on a legal pad. "Yeah, I'll want an official report on that. Thanks, you too. G'bye." He hung up.

"Number goes to a pay phone at 501 Linden Ave. in Carpinteria, and that is where the call to your pager originated," the sheriff told Terry.

"I figured it would be a payphone," Terry said.

"Yeah, me too. But now we know which one. And we have proof that somebody paged you from that number at 3:03 p.m. today."

"It's a start, I guess."

"You think you can take a drive up to Carp, see what's near 501 Linden, scope the area out?"

"Yeah, I could do that," Terry said. "I can do it on my way to Santa Barbara tomorrow. I want to see if I can talk to someone in the sheriff's department up there about Danielle Winfield."

"Hm," Tim grunted. "You'll want to be careful doing that. I'm not sure we can just talk to anybody in that department." He thought a moment. "There is a guy. I don't know him all that well, but he worked with us on a case that crossed the county line a couple of years ago, and I got a good impression. He wanted to solve the case, and he didn't give much a shit about anything else. Lemme see if he's still there."

Tim went back to his Rolodex and found another card, then picked up the phone and dialed again.

"Yeah, Detective Decker in?

"Thanks.

"Detective Decker?

"Hi, this is Sheriff Tim Baker, in Ventura County. Look, I've got a guy here, a friend of mine. He says he was contacted by someone claiming to have information on a couple of murders up your way.

"I know, you don't have many of those. Look, I want to send him up to you so he can tell you about it himself.

"Uh-huh. Yeah, you never know with these things.

"All right, I'll send him up there. Call came from a payphone in Carpinteria. We had it traced. 501 Linden.

"No, it's not a CI. He's a good friend of mine, actually.

"Yeah, name's Terry Cahill.

"Yup, that one. Thanks, Rick.

"You too."

He hung up and turned back to Terry.

"All right, hope you've got a full tank of gas in that ocean liner you're driving," Tim said to Terry. "Detective Decker of the Santa Barbara County Sheriff's Department will meet you at 501 Linden Ave. in Carpinteria as soon as you can get there."

"Tonight?" Terry asked.

"Terry, it's a possible murder. The chances of solving a crime like that diminish drastically if you don't solve it in the first two days after it happened, you know that. Time is everything. He needs to talk to you now."

"I guess I'd better be on my way, then."

"Swing back by here tomorrow morning and give me a report on your conversation with Decker."

"I've got a morning shift at the Reach tomorrow."

"I suppose I could swing by there, then," Tim said. "But don't open me a beer. I'll be on duty."

• • •

Terry topped off the Buick's tank before heading up the 101 to Carpinteria. He'd already burned up more than half a tank just driving around, plus that one trip to Desmond's office in Santa Barbara. With hi-test going for $1.35 a gallon, it cost him 20 bucks to replenish what he'd used. The 455 was smooth and powerful, but thirsty, and the Buick had a 25-gallon tank. He could have saved a few cents a gallon by going to one of the few stations left still selling regular, but the idea of spewing a bunch of tetraethyl lead fumes into the atmosphere did not sit well with Terry. At least it was night time. He could conserve fuel by dropping a couple of windows instead of running the AC.

Five oh-one Linden Ave. turned out to be a convenience store. Terry parked on Linden behind a gray Chevy Caprice, one of the older boxy ones, not one of the new ones that look like beached whales, and saw the payphone sitting out front, but off to the side where there were no windows in the store. A smallish middle-aged man in a corduroy sport coat stood next to the Caprice. Terry got out of his Buick and the man called out.

"You Cahill?" he asked.

"Yeah, Terry Cahill," Terry said. "I have some information I hope you find helpful."

Detective Decker introduced himself and reached into his pocket. Terry thought he was going to show him a badge, but he came out with money. "I don't know what you want for this, but I don't have much on me," Decker said.

"I don't want any money," Terry said, insulted but trying not to show it.

"Just doing your civic duty, huh," Decker said.

"Yes, I am. That, and maybe you can help me out with some information on something I'm looking into."

"So, a trade?"

"No, you get what I have whether you reciprocate or not. We're talking about a fucking murder here."

"All right, all right, calm down," the detective said. "I don't usually get people volunteering information like that, if you know what I mean. Why don't you get in my car, we can talk about it there."

"Mind if I see a badge first?" Terry asked. It was Decker's turn to be insulted, but he showed him his identification anyway. "Thanks." Terry opened the passenger door of the Caprice and slid in.

"Put your seatbelt on," Decker said, starting the car.

Terry buckled up and Decker dropped the car into gear and pulled away from the curb. He drove around slowly as Terry told him just the very basics of the story he was investigating about the Santa Barbara Boys, and then told him a somewhat sanitized version of his encounter with Scott Keener and the conversation he'd had today with the man who didn't want to be identified. When he was done, Decker looped back around to Linden and parked his undercover cruiser behind Terry's Buick. He sat for a moment thinking before speaking.

"You used to be a reporter for the *VC Monitor,* didn't you?" Decker said.

"Yes," Terry responded. "I was fired a couple of weeks ago. Long story."

"Yeah, I used to see your byline there. Haven't seen it lately." He sat there thinking again, staring out the windshield in front of him toward the beach just a few dozen yards away. "Sheriff Baker seems to trust you. Called you a friend, even."

"I know. I was there when he made the call."

"OK. I don't know you for shit, but I've worked with Baker, and I like him. He says you're OK, I'll trust him and you. For now."

"Look, what you do with this is up to you now. I'm not trying to tell you how to do your job. But I would appreciate it if you could tell me a little something about Danielle Winfield. So would Sheriff Baker."

"Not his jurisdiction," Decker said.

"But it is most likely tied to a crime that is within his jurisdiction."

"Like what?"

"Trust is a two-way street."

"All right, let me look into the case files. I'll get back to you with more details. But here's what I remember off the top of my head, OK. Winfield was a surfer from Venice Beach, a professional. Apparently a pretty good one. It was during the '84 Olympics, and all the beaches down there were jammed up with tourists, from Malibu to San Pedro. According to her roommate, she came up here to try out Rincon, and to get away from all the crowds in LA. The roommate was supposed to go with her, but for some reason Winfield ended up on the beach alone.

"A group of surfers found her body washed up on the shore, already dead. It looked like an accident. I think the coroner ruled that she had slipped off her board and hit her head on it on the way down. The board knocked her unconscious, and she drowned in the surf."

"You said, 'it *looked* like an accident.' Why do I get the impression that you never bought that?"

"Because she was a championship surfer, and the waves weren't all that big that day. I *don't* fucking buy it. It smells wrong. But the only evidence there was fit that story well enough, and nothing ever came up to contradict it. Besides, it wasn't my case."

"Whose case was it?" Terry asked.

"Uh-uh. I don't trust you that much yet. Like I said, I'll do some digging around and get back to you."

"Meaning part of that digging around will be looking at me."

"You're not dumb, I'll give you that," Decker said.

"That's fine. Do what you must. But when you're done, I'd like to get the names of the surfers who found her. Also the roommate, and any contact info you have on, what, her, I'm guessing."

"Like I said, I'll get back to you."

"I guess I'd better give you my card, then," Terry said. He handed Decker one of his old business cards. "The pager number is still good. You can reach me that way." Decker handed Terry one of his own cards.

"If you think of anything else ..." Decker said.

"Yeah, I'll be sure to reach out."

"Will you be willing to testify in court if anything comes of this?"

"Of course."

"Civic duty, huh."

"A sense of justice is how I would put it."

Terry got out of the cruiser and went back toward his Buick.

24

Momentum

Sheriff Baker met with Terry at 11 a.m. at the Beam Reach. Terry saw him walk in and poured a cup of coffee for him, black. For a bar, the Reach actually had pretty good coffee. Not that very many of the patrons drank it.

"You didn't go up there and kick his ass, did you?" Tim asked.

"Nah, he's a cop," Terry replied. "I bribed him with donuts instead."

"Always works on me. You got any left?"

Terry pulled a box of Winchell's from under the bar and set it down in front of the sheriff. Tim took a plain glazed, and Terry selected a chocolate-covered with sprinkles. They both paused conversation long enough to savor their first bites. Terry poured a coffee for himself, and began telling Tim what he'd learned from Detective Decker the night before.

"You think they got away with a murder seven years ago?" Tim asked.

"I strongly suspect it," Terry said. "Like Decker said, she was a championship surfer out there on a relatively calm day. It could have been an accident, but he doesn't seem to think so, and I don't either."

"Yeah, it feels kinda wrong." Tim thought for a moment. "I keep coming back to that phone call yesterday. We need to find out who he was. Any clues at the location."

"Sort of. I could see why he picked that location. It's a little market. The phones are off to the side of the building, away from the windows in front. He could have approached the phones, made his call, and left all without being seen from the store. To anyone driving by, he'd just be someone using the payphone. Across the street is a big warehouse, looks abandoned, no windows. Nobody could have gotten a very close look at him. Maybe he lives or works in the area, but I don't have much to go on for finding out."

"We can start off with the assumption that he's one of the Santa Barbara Boys gang."

"That seems likely."

"And that the murder of Scott Keener triggered him somehow, to the point where he wants revenge, or justice."

Hearing Keener's name again shook a memory loose for Terry. Something clicked into place. He told Tim to wait a second and ran out to his Buick in the marina parking lot. He hadn't had the car long enough to clutter it up, but in the glovebox he found what he was looking for. He brought the reporter's notepad back in to the Reach and started flipping through the pages, looking for the notes he'd made yesterday at the library.

"Here it is," Terry said. "I can't believe I didn't see it yesterday."

"You plan on sharing with me?" Tim asked.

"I found an article from about 12 years ago about surfers in Santa Barbara County when I was looking up info on Dewey Michaels. The article had a picture of a group of guys, including Michaels. I wrote all their names down. Here it is: Bradley Keane. One of the original Santa Barbara Boys."

"Keane, Keener? I see the similarity, but I don't get where you're going with it."

"Newspapers fuck up names all the time. It's embarrassing, but true. Especially in captions, because the notes from those come from the photographers, and they don't always ask the subjects to spell their names out."

"So maybe this guy said 'Keener,' but the photographer heard 'Keane.' I dunno, it sounds like a long shot."

"We could find out, though. Look up records for Bradley Keane and Bradley Keener, see which one hits."

Sheriff Baker's cop instinct started twinging on the idea. "OK, I'll look into that. You may be onto something."

"What do you want to bet that he's related to Scott Keener?"

"Maybe a brother," Tim said.

"Sounds likely. What would cause you to turn against a group of guys you'd been friends with for more than a decade? People who may be tied to you by shared criminal activity."

"If they killed my brother, that'd do it."

"Yeah, me too. And I don't even like any of my brothers."

• • •

Up in Santa Barbara, Detective Decker was at his desk bright and early even though it was a Saturday morning. He had three potential homicides to look into, and he didn't plan on resting much until he knew what was going on. He had barely sat down when his desk phone rang. He answered. It was Terry Cahill on the other end.

"Morning, detective," Cahill said. "I think I have something you might want to check out."

"Well, don't keep me waiting, Cahill," Decker said.

"I have a hunch about who called me on the Keener murder."

"We don't know it's a murder yet, and a hunch from someone I don't know isn't a whole lot to go on."

"Yeah, well, do you want it or not? You told me to call you if I thought of anything."

"Yeah, yeah, what is your hunch, Cahill?"

"Keener had an older brother, didn't he?"

"Yeah, a Bradley Keener. Noted as Scott's next of kin. Why?"

"His name came up when I was looking into the Santa Barbara Boys surf gang. Found him in an article from back about 12 years ago. Scott Keener was one of them, too."

"So, Keener liked to surf. His brother liked to surf, too. Hell, this is coastal California. You can't throw a rock without hitting someone who likes to surf. You know, I think that whole surf gang angle is a bunch of horseshit blown all out of proportion by the press. We've never been able to even prove they really exist. Some surfers are assholes. That's probably all it is. We got no hard evidence saying they're organized."

"Scott Keener and his buddies sure tried to kick my ass when I went to go surfing on Rincon. Somebody put Brandon Capriani in a coma for doing the same. I'd say there's more than just press horseshit there, detective." Terry paused, and Decker left the silence untouched.

"Look, both Keeners were part of a group of surfers who spent time at Rincon. I have my own personal experience with this group being violently opposed to other people surfing at Rincon. Then I get a tip about Scott Keener being murdered. Can we at least agree that that tip most likely came from someone who was familiar with both the victim and this group of surfers?"

"OK, for the sake of argument, let's say you're right. Then what?"

"Let's say this group of surfers is connected through criminal endeavors, say, the assault of people trying to surf at Rincon. Suppose you're a member of this group. What would cause you to rat them out?"

"You mean like if they killed my brother?"

"Yeah, I mean exactly like if they killed your brother."

"I don't even like my brother."

"Neither do I."

"You don't even know my bother."

"Yeah, but if he's anything like you, he's a first-rate prick."

"OK, it's a motive. It's thin, but it's all we've got to go on from that angle."

Terry noticed it was "we" now, and wondered if it was a slip of the tongue.

"So you're going to check out the brother?" Terry asked.

"I was going to interview him anyway. Now I have a couple more tells to look for when I do. So, thanks, Cahill. I might even share some of what I find out from him."

"All right, thanks, detective."

"Hey, Cahill? You know the roommate? You said you wanted to talk to her, right?"

"Yeah."

"I tracked her down for you. Anna Henley, well, Anna Preston now. Seems she got married. You're in luck. She lives in Camarillo now, so you won't have to drive that piece of shit of yours all the way down to Venice." Decker gave Terry an address on Via Latina Drive, where Danielle Winfield's former roommate now lived.

"OK, got it," Terry said. "Thanks again, detective."

"No problem. Look, I don't think you're going to find anything there, but if you do ..."

"I'll be sure to share it with you."

Decker hung up the phone. It was only then that he noticed he wasn't alone in the office. Deputy Kirkham was there hovering around the coffee machine. Decker got up and pretended he needed a cup too.

"Hey, Kerry," Decker said. "Didn't know you were on-duty today."

"Yeah, I traded shifts with Burt. He had tickets to a Dodger game today, so he's taking the next two shifts I don't want." Deputy Kirkham grinned.

"Giving up a Saturday this time of year? You surf, don't you?"

"Eh, not as much as I used to. You know how it is, time and all."

"You ever surf Rincon?"

Kirkham laughed. "Rick, I've surfed every beach between Pismo and San Diego, and more than once."

"Maybe you can help me out. You ever been beat up for trying to surf on an unfamiliar beach?"

"Not too many people have tried to beat me up for anything, and the few who did regretted it, I'll tell you that much."

Yeah, yeah, I get it, you're a real tough guy, Decker thought, trying not to roll his eyes. Every police department across the country had a few like that.

"So you've never run into that kind of thing, at Rincon or anywhere else?" Decker asked.

Kirkham shrugged. "Some surfers can be pretty territorial, I guess. I've been knocked off my board a few times, stuff like that. Something that could always be called an accident. But, you know, I think they see me and see a guy who'll give right back. I think the guys who pull that stuff are usually pussies. They might pick on someone if they think he's weaker, but I'm not weaker. Sorry. And if you're working some kind of angle on that Santa Barbara Boys shit, well, I think that's just a bunch of crap to sell newspapers and scare people. What I've seen, there's nothing to that."

"OK, I was just checking. You're the only guy I know around here who surfs, so I thought I'd ask. Thanks."

"Sure thing," Kirkham said. "I should go out on patrol now."

Decker waited until Kirkham left, then started poking around the old case files for the Winfield accident. The investigation was only cursory. But it wasn't the report that was first caught his attention; it was the signature of the responding officer: Deputy Kirkham. Decker thought about that for a moment. The department wasn't all that big. Still, what were the chances?

The next thing that jumped out at him was the name of one of the surfers who had dragged Winfield out of the water: Jonathan Abernathy.

Decker understood that coincidences could happen. Sometimes they were even uncanny. But when they started stacking up like this, it made him uneasy.

He picked back up with what was in the file. There was a report from the ME concluding it was an accidental death, and a basic incident report filed, and not much of anything else. The x-rays of Winfield's cracked skull were not included, but with some luck they may be in the records at the coroner's office across the 101 from the sheriff's office. Decker slipped the case documents into another folder he'd brought in with him and left the records room.

Decker had drawn the Keener case on the supposition that it was a suicide, exactly as it looked. Keener had been found on a Friday evening, too late for the county ME to do anything with the body. He had the corpse sent to Dr. Kreutz over at St. Francis for autopsy. Part of the reason was simple expediency: He wanted the autopsy performed sooner rather than later, and knew the county ME didn't like coming in on weekends.

But there was something else, too. He was beginning to not trust the county ME. He didn't think so much that the ME was crooked as he was sloppy. Or maybe that was too harsh. Santa Barbara County Medical Examiner would be a pretty cushy job, as far as such jobs go. Most of the deaths that would be investigated would result from car accidents. There was the occasional drowning, and a very rare overdose here and there. But very few homicides. Decker knew that only about a fourth of all deaths in the county warranted an autopsy. Sheriff-Coroner Ray Fields trusted the ME, Decker knew, but sheriff-coroner was as much a political position as it was a law-enforcement job. It didn't exactly pay dividends to suggest to the mostly wealthy voters of Santa Barbara County that their upscale hamlets and sleepy beach towns far from LA might not be as safe as they thought they were.

He decided he'd go by the coroner's office and try to get the Winfield x-rays on his way to see Dr. Kreutz. He wanted to see what Kreutz had learned on the Keener autopsy anyway. But he also wanted the doc to give him a second opinion on Winfield.

There was only one clerk working at the coroner's office on weekends, and Decker knew that during the lunch hour the office would be left unattended. He wanted to get there just before lunch, both so that the office wouldn't be locked, and so that hopefully the clerk would be in a hurry to get him out of there and not think too hard about the story Decker was about to give her.

Decker eased his unmarked Caprice into the parking lot of the coroner's building at 10 minutes to noon. The clerk on duty was already watching the clock. Decker didn't blame her. It was probably a pretty boring day. He showed his ID and asked for the Winfield file, and, to his mild surprise, the clerk didn't even ask him why he wanted it. She just told him to wait there and went back to the records room to retrieve it.

The clerk brought back the file, and Decker opened the folder to make sure the x-rays were there. He thanked the clerk, turned, and walked out the door carrying the file with him.

It was only a short drive back across the 101 to St. Francis from the coroner's building. He had phoned ahead and asked Dr. Kreutz to meet him there so he could hear about the Keener autopsy. He figured he'd ask her opinion about the coroner's report on Winfield while he was there.

Dr. Kreutz met Detective Decker in her office. She was making notes on a small pad of paper when he walked in. Decker wondered if it was something about the autopsy, but the truth was far less interesting: She was writing down her lunch order. She saw the file folder in his hand and wondered what that was about.

"Good afternoon, detective," Dr. Kreutz said. "Please have a seat." Decker sat down in one of the two chairs in front of her desk. "You bring something new for me?"

"I was hoping you'd take a look at these," Decker said, putting the folder on her desk. "From an old case, seven years ago. Officially deemed 'accidental.' I got a funny feeling about it."

"Detective, I appreciate your apparent faith in my abilities, but I can't necessarily go over every case of suspicious death in the county."

"This might be connected to Abernathy and Keener," he said. "I understand if you can't ..."

"You think Abernathy and Keener are connected?" she asked, her interest now piqued. She reached for the Winfield file.

"Well, maybe. My gut says they are. I'd bet a month's pay that you're going to tell me that Keener was not a suicide, and if that's the case, I think he's linked to the Abernathy thing." He didn't mention Abernathy's connection to Winfield's death.

"OK, points scored. You're right: I'm ruling Keener as a homicide, not a suicide."

"Why?

Kreutz picked up a photo from her desk and handed it over to Decker. "Mainly this," she said. "That's a picture of the back of Keener's head, after shaving it." The image showed a bruise roughly the size and shape of a man's fist.

"You think someone hit him on the back of the head, knocked him out, and made it look like a suicide?" Decker asked.

"Not exactly. I think someone grabbed him by the hair on the back of the head and used it as a handle to slam his forehead into the front of the car he supposedly fell on." She used a pencil as a pointer and showed the detective what she was talking about.

"See the redness around the individual hair follicles?" she asked. Decker nodded" That indicates the the hairs were pulled with some degree of force. Then notice the shape of the bruise. It's hard to tell, but there are parts where the trauma is more pronounced. You can almost make out four vertical lines across the width of it. Those, I suspect, are from fingers. Then underneath that is a long horizontal line. That would be from the palm

"When you shove someone's head into something in that fashion, you get two marks, two different injuries, basically. The first, on his forehead, obviously came from whatever he was shoved into. That we were meant to see. But when the front of the head impacts, the back of the head is impacted as well, by whatever is propelling it. In this case, a man's fist. It's not quite like hitting a piece of clay, but it still leaves a definable impression."

"You say it's a man?"

"The size would be unusually large for a woman's hand."

"I see," Decker said. "Anything else?"

"An inspection of the victim's lung tissue suggests he wasn't breathing very deeply at the time of death. Concentrations of carbon monoxide and unburned hydrocarbons were much lower in the deep part of the lungs than they were at the upper parts. It doesn't necessarily prove he didn't kill himself, but it's not what I expect to see in this kind of suicide. Typically the victims of intentional carbon monoxide self-poisoning breathe deeply, at least at first, to speed the process. No turning back, you see."

Both the doctor and the cop found that tidbit depressing.

"There are other indications, as well," Kreutz continued. "But they get pretty technical. If you want, you can read it all in my report. But the takeaway is that Keener was deliberately killed by another person. It's a homicide."

Decker was expecting the news, but it still sent a chill through him. Two murders in the span of just a few days. Both victims rumored to be members of a local surfing club. Surely they knew of each other, at the very least. *What's going on here?* the detective thought.

"So what's this one about?" Kreutz asked, opening the file.

"Danielle Winfield. She was a professional surfer, won a couple of championships. Seven years ago she comes up here to surf Rincon, and ends up drowning. Coroner ruled it an accident, said she slipped and fell off her board, the board hit her on the head and knocked her out, and she drowned. I've got my own suspicions, but I want to get a read on it from you, if you don't mind."

The doctor was already looking at the report. She pulled out the x-ray and held it up to get some light behind it.

"OK, that's interesting," she said.

"See something?"

"Well, for one, we've got another suspicious accidental death, and it also involves a head injury."

"Yeah, that bugs me too."

"But look at the shape of the skull fracture. Again, it's not what I expect to see in this kind of accident."

"You'll have to explain for me, doc."

"OK, again, this isn't definitive. But in this kind of mishap, I expect to see that she hit her head on the flat of the board. But that's not what happened here. If this fracture was caused by a surfboard, it would have to be the edge of the board that struck her, not the flat."

"How can you tell that?"

"The head is basically a spherical object. When it impacts with something flat, it fractures in a radial pattern. Imagine dropping a ball of clay on the pavement. It'll be flat on the bottom, where it strikes, right? The head will pretty much do the same thing. You can see it in the radial pattern made by the fracture."

She held the x-ray up so Decker could see it, and pointed at the hairline fracture on the back of Winfield's skull. It was shaped like a line with a slight curve to it.

"This doesn't look like that at all. This is a fracture caused by an impact with something oblong and thin relative to the skull. Could have been a baseball bat, or any number of things. If it was a surfboard, it was the edge of the board. Now, that can happen. All kinds of things can happen out there on the water. But usually, when a surfer falls off a board and hits their head on it, they hit their face or the back of their head on flat part of the board. The board's buoyancy tends to keep it oriented that way. Sometimes they do strike their heads on the edge of the board, but in those cases the injury is typically to the side of the head, not the back. Either they fall down backwards and hit the backs of their heads on the flat of the board, they fall forward and hit their face on the flat, or they slide off the side and strike the sides of their heads on the edge of their boards. None of this is conclusive, of course, but I'm seeing several patterns here and I don't like it.

"You said Keener and Abernathy were connected? Was Keener a surfer too?"

"Yeah, doc," Decker said. "He most likely belonged to the same surfing club as Abernathy, too."

"Three surfers. At least two homicides somewhat clumsily disguised as something else. And a third death that was ruled accidental, but looks at least a little unusual."

"Yeah. I don't like it."

"Neither do I," Kreutz said. "You mind if I hold onto the Winfield file and go over the report more thoroughly?

"I was hoping you would."

"Give me the rest of the weekend with it, if you can, detective."

"Thank you, doctor."

25

Hanging Out

A group of Santa Barbara Boys were hanging out at Rincon Beach. None of them were surfing, and half of them hadn't even gone to the pretense of bringing their boards with them. The shark attacks had them spooked pretty well, and while some of them talked tough within the group, everybody knew that nobody would be surfing anytime soon.

Don Harris was shooting the shit with Jeremy Dodd and Mike Tonin when he was interrupted.

"Holy shit!" Dodd said, pointing out toward the water. "Lookit that!"

At first they thought the fins belonged to dolphins, as it wasn't unusual to see them playing in the surf. But the shape was wrong, the color not quite right.

"There's gotta be at least a dozen of the bastards out there." Dodd said.

"Are those ..." Tonin trailed off.

"Yeah. They're fuckin' sharks."

"Jesus Christ!" Harris said.

• • •

It was late, after hours, and Wendy and Terry had just finished closing the Beam Reach. She popped open a Dos Equis for herself, sans lime, and offered Terry a beer too.

"So, that slip you were asking about?" Wendy said.

"Oh, yeah," Terry said. "You find out who's renting it?"

"Uh-huh. It belongs to a Jake and Brenda Sims, out of Somis."

"Sims?" Terry thought of Dave Sims. The address the sheriff had given him was in Somis too. Couldn't be a coincidence.

"That's what the harbormaster told me."

"How did you get him to tell you?"

"I batted my eyelashes and looked real pretty," she said. "OK, actually, after I talked to you, I went over to that slip and checked it out. There was a nice Chris-Craft in there, no name. So I told the harbormaster I was following a Chris-Craft in the other day, and one of their fenders fell off and I netted it. Wanted to know who to give it back to."

"Slick," Terry said admiringly. "Thanks for getting that for me."

"No big deal, except you owe me now. You need to get out of here or anything?" she asked.

"No, I got no plans other than crashing, but I'm not tired now," he said, opening his can of Schlitz. "Why?"

"I just wanted to know if you wanted to hang out for a little while. I'm not tired either, and I don't feel like being alone."

"Yeah, OK. I'll stick around. Kinda nice having the place to ourselves, isn't it?"

"I like it too. The place feels different late at night, after everyone's gone and it's all been cleaned up." She took a swig of beer, then pointed at the can in Terry's hand. "I don't know how the hell you can drink that shit."

"It's really all the same to me," he said, taking his own pull. "Mallory, my ex, er, almost ex-wife. She used to say the same thing. She'd buy Heineken, usually. Sometimes other brands, but always some kind of

European import. I'd drink it. I mean, what the hell, right? But the biggest difference to me was that it cost almost three times as much."

Terry reflected for a moment, and Wendy just looked at him, seemingly lost in thought.

"I guess there's more to it than that," he continued. "I mean, my dad always drank the cheapest beer he could find. He was an Army guy, didn't make a ton of money. But he also grew up when these beers were what everybody drank, y'know? Then years later I was in the Army myself. Spent the better part of three years sitting on my ass in a guard shack at the edge of a base in Würzburg, a little hick town in Germany.

"In a lot of ways, the Germans could be perfectly nice people. But they could be insufferably smug about some things. Beer was one of those things. To hear them tell it, the stuff we drank over here wasn't even the same thing as the beer they had over there. But I had plenty of their beer, and it just wasn't all that different. Used to really get under my skin. To get under theirs, I made a habit of reminding them that all the guys who started the big American breweries, you know, Joseph Schlitz, Gottlieb Pabst, Adolph Coors, Frederick Miller, Eberhard Anheuser and Adolphus Busch, they were all Germans. Used to really piss them off.

"Anyway, the whole time I was over there, I'd drink their beer when all I really wanted was a Schlitz. So when I got out of the Army and moved back stateside, I started drinking the same kind of beers my dad drank. Only by then they were considered 'cheap' beers. But that just made them more appealing to me. Why would I want to spend extra money on something I'm just going to piss out in a couple hours anyway?"

"Interesting perspective," Wendy said, finishing off her Dos Equis. "I think you've convinced me." She went back to the beer fridge and got two cans of Schlitz this time, handing one to Terry, who finished off the can he was working on.

She opened her can and took a big sip, then immediately grimaced.

"Same thing, my black ass," she said. "This shit is nasty."

"You get used to it after a while, I guess."

"I need something to get this taste out of my mouth. Hey, you hungry?"

Terry was, in fact, kinda hungry. "Yeah, I could eat," he said. "Probably shouldn't at this hour, but what the hell."

"I could get the fryer going, do up some mozzarella sticks, onion rings, something?"

"Yeah, we could do that. What's in that kitchen back there, anyway?"

"Just all the shit we have on the menu here. Mostly greasy bar food. We could make club sandwiches." They were walking back to the bar's kitchen, passing through the swinging doors.

"You have bacon?"

"Hell yeah, we have bacon."

Terry started snooping around, picking things up, looking at labels. "Yeah, I think you've got everything here," he said almost to himself.

"Everything would be a stretch," Wendy said.

"Sorry, I meant everything I'd need to make a chili."

"You make chili?"

"Yeah, homemade. My own recipe and everything."

"How long does it take?"

"Hour and a half, maybe two hours. Think you can hold out that long?"

"I probably can if I break out some chips and salsa while you're cooking."

"All right, let's do this," Terry said. "I miss cooking, anyway. The galley on *Easy Goer* is pretty small." He found a frying pan and put five strips of bacon in it, setting the flame to medium. Then he put a large pot on the burner next to it and started browning ground beef in a bit of olive oil.

"Anything I can do to help?" Wendy asked.

"If you want, you can chop up the bacon when it's done. We want it cooked, but not crispy."

"Bacon in chili? I think I'm in love already."

"I'll need some red wine, too. Got any open bottles left from tonight?"

Terry kept putting ingredients together for his chili until all there was left to do was let it cook down. He and Wendy continued to drink, tying on a pretty good buzz as the chili simmered and filled the kitchen of the Beam Reach with an aroma almost as intoxicating as the liquor on the bar's shelves.

• • •

That same night, as Terry was cooking his chili in the bar's kitchen and getting tipsy with Wendy, Dave Sims was loading the last of his lobster cages onto his parents' Chris-Craft. He trolled out of the marina as usual before starting the boat's inboard and heading for Rincon Point.

He enjoyed the night air on the water, especially once the boat picked up enough speed for the wind to blow the stink of his cargo behind him like a wake in the air. So far, things were going as they always had for him. The trips had become a comfortable routine.

The first sign of something out of the ordinary for this outing came as he neared his destination. The radar had picked up what looked like a small vessel heading out to sea from the general direction of the Santa Barbara Harbor. Sims throttled back to 10 knots and listened, keeping his eye on the radar screen. The vessel turned south toward Rincon. After a few minutes the boat was close enough for Sims to hear its engines. Sounded like a pair of powerful outboards to him.

He knew that if it was some kind of patrol boat, he'd have some explaining to do. But it didn't feel like that to him. The boat was on a straight course, and moving fairly fast, but it wasn't headed straight for him. He estimated that if he kept going at his current speed and heading, he'd cross the other boat's wake maybe a quarter mile or so behind it.

Curiosity got the better of him. He changed his heading slightly, so that he would still cross the other boat's path behind it, but not quite as far away. He also throttled back again to just above idle hoping to quiet his MerCruiser 454 inboard enough that its sound would be drowned out by the noise of the other boat's outboards, at least to whomever was piloting the other boat.

Sims wasn't sure exactly why he did this. Part of him wanted to know who this was, what this other boat was doing at this hour. Part of him thought it might be best to not be heading directly for the area where he'd been dropping shark bait off the beach.

He saw the boat silhouetted against the moonlight and altered his course again so that he'd be following it. It looked like a fishing boat. Not a commercial one, but a small sport-fishing vessel, maybe a Boston Whaler. The pilot of the other boat hadn't seemed to notice Sims yet. They were roughly three miles off shore by Sims's estimate when the boat cut throttle and began drifting down to a stop. Sims kept idling forward at a speed of 2 knots, trying to get just a little closer to the fishing boat.

He heard a big splash as something heavy fell, or was dropped, into the ocean. It didn't sound like an anchor, and the water here was too deep for one anyway if Sims remembered his charts correctly. There was a pair of marine binoculars stowed in one of the compartments under the seats of the Chris-Craft, and Sims pulled them out, bringing them to his eyes.

There wasn't a lot of light, but it was enough for Sims to catch the name painted in gold leaf on the stern. *Artemis.*

Someone's a fan of mythology, Sims thought.

He heard the outboards fire back up on *Artemis*, and watched it make a big looping turn starboard, apparently heading back in the direction of Rincon and the intended drop zone for Sims's cargo. It was a somewhat lucky break for Sims, as he had been looming off the fishing boat's port side. Once the boat was far enough away, he dumped the pig heads and entrails out of the lobster cages and into the ocean. He was spooked out of his mission for the night. He throttled up his own engine to head back to Ventura. He had kept the cages, though. He could always come back the next night and do it then, he figured.

• • •

The killer hadn't spotted Sims shadowing him. He wasn't much of a boatsman, and he didn't think anyone would be out at that hour to see him anyway. Brad Keener's body sank into the ocean without ceremony, wrapped in a fishing net and dragged down by a pair of 10-kg. iron weights from a set of barbells. Maybe the sharks would get this one too.

He'd taken a different tack in the killing of the elder Keener brother, mainly because he felt that another body in Santa Barbara County might be one too many. He thought he was safe, but didn't want to take unnecessary chances. He knew that the local cops were poking around into things, and at the very least didn't want to give them any more evidence.

Keener's disappearance would attract some attention, of course, but without a body no one would know for sure what had happened.

What had happened was the killer lured Keener outside in the dark parking lot of Shockley's Tavern with a promise of information about his brother's murder. When Keener arrived, the killer sneaked up behind him and hit him with a stun gun. He then bound Keener's hands and pulled a plastic bag over his head, holding it there until Keener had suffocated. Then he stuffed the body in the back of Keener's SUV, drove to the harbor, and struggled to get the corpse onto *Artemis*.

The killer didn't own the boat. In fact, it had belonged to his most recent victim. The keys were on the ring in his pocket, same as his car keys. The fishing net and the weights had been in the trunk of the killer's car. Once he'd gotten the body aboard and prepped for burial at sea, he swiped a plastic kayak from a rack by the dock, lashed it to the railing on

Artemis, then took the boat out of the harbor and went out toward Rincon Point.

He dumped Keener, then set a course back to shore before turning north toward Carpinteria. About a quarter mile off the coast, he once again shut down the two outboard motors and absent-mindedly pocketed the keys. He pulled the ocean kayak off the deck, dropped it into the water, and climbed in.

The killer paddled away in the kayak, leaving *Artemis* to drift on the calm water. Once on shore, he dragged the kayak onto the beach behind him in an attempt to obscure his footprints in the sand. He dropped the kayak behind him and walked up Linden Avenue to Carpinteria Avenue, where he'd parked his car. He didn't feel Keener's keys slide out of his pocket and into the crack between the seat and the console as he sat down.

• • •

By the time the chili was ready, Terry and Wendy were well and truly drunk. And hungry. He topped the steaming bowls with sharp cheddar cheese, and handed one to Wendy. He poured the rest of the red wine he'd used in the chili into two wine glasses, and handed one of those to Wendy as well.

"Fuckin' A, Terry," she said after a couple of bites. "This is fucking delicious."

"Thanks," he said around his own mouthful of chili.

"I'm serious, I could sell this. Add it to the menu here. You think you could teach the kitchen staff how to make it?"

"I'll tell you what," Terry said after considering for a few seconds. "I don't want to share my recipe, but if you want to sell it here, I'll come in early and make a batch myself in the mornings."

"What about when I run out?"

"Then you can't sell any more that day, and demand goes up for the next day's batch. It's how they do barbecue in Texas, and those places are never hurting for business."

"OK. Deal."

They clinked glasses to seal it.

"I'm gonna put the leftovers in the fridge. Start selling it by the mug tomorrow."

26

Witnesses

Terry and Wendy woke up that morning on opposite sides of a booth in the Beam Reach. They had passed out there after drinking into the wee hours. Terry peeled himself off the naugahyde upholstery and the noise of it roused Wendy, who had fallen asleep with her face on the table.

"Jesus, how much did we end up drinking last night?" she said.

"We could count the empties if we really want to know. Do you?"

"No."

"Me either," Terry said.

She got up and went back to her office, where she kept a bottle of aspirin in a small first-aid kit. Terry went behind the bar and got some coffee going. Wendy came back, dropped two aspirin in Terry's hand, and opened a Dos Equis. After washing the pills down with the beer, she handed the bottle to Terry, who did the same.

"Hair of the dog," Terry said.

"If this hangover were a dog, I'd put it to sleep," she replied.

"We need some donuts."

"We do, but I ain't going to get them."

"I could fry up some eggs." The suggestion made Wendy gag, and she punched him on the arm. "I'll take that as a 'no' then." They settled for plain wheat toast and the coffee.

Terry knew he'd feel at least a little better after a shower, so when they were done with their toast and coffee he said goodbye and walked over to *Easy Goer* to retrieve his shower bag.

• • •

That morning, a young camper woke up with the sunrise in his truck parked at the Carpinteria State Beach camping grounds. He shrugged off his sleeping bag to go out and walk the beach, where he found a plastic yellow kayak unattended. He looked around and saw nobody. The camper dragged the kayak off to his truck thinking, *Finders keepers.*

• • •

Freshly out of a steaming hot shower, the aspirin and caffeine starting to kick in, Terry was feeling better than he had upon waking up in the bar he'd drank all night in. It was time to get the day started in a productive direction.

He knew he needed to talk to Anna Preston, Winfield's former roommate. He couldn't shake the feeling that something was there, maybe even the key to the whole thing. Detective Decker had given him a name and an address, but no phone number. Terry had no idea whether he'd catch her at home or not, but decided the only thing to do would be to drive down to Camarillo and find out. Face-to-face conversations were better for getting a story out of someone anyway, in his experience.

• • •

A Coast Guard helicopter had spotted *Artemis* on the water a couple of miles south of where it had been abandoned by the killer, and called it in. The boat had no below-deck space and the cockpit was open, so it was immediately clear that no one was on-board. The spotter on the helo began looking for someone in the water, thinking maybe the boat's occupant, or occupants, had fallen overboard. But nobody was visible on the water.

A small Coast Guard response boat was dispatched out to get a closer look. Its crew didn't have any better luck in finding anybody, but they were able to board the boat. They found it to be in operational condition as far as they could tell at a glance. The tanks had fuel, and there was nothing obviously wrong with the vessel. But there were no keys in it.

The Coast Guard crew attached a tow rope to *Artemis* and towed it back in to their base. The boat was now a potential crime scene. It would be torn apart and searched for drugs. And human blood.

• • •

Billy Newhouse was pissed. He had just gotten off the phone with one of his bartenders, who was wondering who the hell was going to open Shockley's Tavern and let him in. Billy's partner, the other half-owner of Shockley's, Brad Keener, was supposed to be there, but he hadn't shown up and the bartender couldn't get him on the phone.

Goddamned Bradley! Newhouse fumed to himself. *If he's on that fucking fishing boat of his, I'm gonna superglue his nuts to his leg.*

Newhouse was not particularly sensitive to the fact that his partner had just lost a brother to an apparent suicide. The younger Keener was a weasely little prick as far as Newhouse was concerned, and his older brother a goddamned flake. He was upset that he'd have to drive all the way down to Carpinteria to open the bar, which Brad had agreed to do this week since Newhouse was in a not insignificant amount of pain thanks to his broken ribs. Now he'd have to go down there and maybe even lift shit, which hurt like hell. He grumbled as he got his keys.

He was still in a foul mood after having opened Shockley's, supervising the morning staff, when Detective Decker walked into the place.

"I'm looking for Brad Keener," Decker said by way of greeting.

"Me too," Newhouse said. "Good luck finding the shithead."

"I take it he's not in?"

"He was supposed to be. And I'm supposed to be in my La-Z-Boy taking it easy."

"He did just lose his brother, you know," Decker said.

"Life is tough all over," Newhouse replied without sympathy.

Decker didn't like the man he was talking to. Didn't like his attitude, didn't like the way he was speaking to an officer of the law, didn't like the look on his face. He decided to put the screws to him and see what fell out.

"How long have you known Brad Keener, Mr., uh, what is your name, sir?" Decker asked in his second-most intimidating cop voice.

"Bill Newhouse. Am I in trouble here?"

"You could be. Will be if you don't answer my questions. How long, Mr. Newhouse?"

"Since college. We met at USC, same graduating class."

"I take it that means you knew his brother, Scott, too. Is that right?"

"Not really. I mean, I knew both of them. Didn't really hang out with Scott, though. He was younger. I didn't grow up here like the rest of the guys."

"Rest of the guys?"

"Oh, just the other guys Brad hangs out with. Surfers, mostly."

"You surf with them""

"Sometimes. I'm not as into it as they are. I grew up in Riverside. Not a lot of beachfront there, you know."

"You know why Scott would want to kill himself?"

"No. Like I said, I mostly knew Brad. What's with all the questions?"

"What about enemies? You know anyone maybe had it in for either of them?"

"No, man! I don't know anything about that. What's going on here?"

"Do you know where I can find Brad Keener?"

"I can think of four possibilities: He's either at home, or he crashed at some chick's place, or he's on the beach surfing, or he's out on that damned boat of his. That's the best I can give you, officer."

"Detective," Decker said.

"Whatever."

"And I don't think he's at home, Mr. Newhouse. I've already been by there this morning. His car wasn't there, and nobody answered the door."

"Well, try the other options then."

"I will. You happen to know the name of his boat?"

"*Artemis*. It's a little Boston Whaler. Keeps it at the harbor in Santa Barbara."

Decker left Shockley's to head back up to Santa Barbara. He stopped at the station on the way to the harbor, and found message slips on his desk. The Coast Guard was looking for Brad Keener too. Instead of calling them back, he went back out to his Caprice and drove to the Coast Guard base at the Santa Barbara harbor.

He took the 101 South to Castillo Street, then made a right on Shoreline Drive. The Coast Guard station was right there at the west end of the marina. Decker parked his undercover car and went over to the station. He was met inside by a master chief named Donnelly. He introduced himself and told Donnelly why he was there.

"We don't have much to go on," Donnelly said. "We found the boat apparently abandoned, drifting approximately eight miles south of the harbor. Didn't see anyone near it, so we towed it in. We had a team go through it, thinking maybe it was a drug thing gone wrong, but so far, nothing. No drugs. We found some small traces of blood, but it's a fishing boat, so there's a good chance that it's not human.

"Anyway, we looked up the boat's registration, found out whose it was, and called you. Have you been able to locate Mr. Keener?"

"No, I haven't. And that bothers me, because I was already looking for him before you tried to contact me."

The detective and the master chief shared a knowing look. Neither of them liked the direction this was headed.

Decker went back to his car and used the radio to call in. He asked the dispatcher to connect with the DMV to find Brad Keener's vehicle registration. She radioed back five minutes later with a license plate number and a description of the vehicle. It was listed as a blue 1989 Dodge Ramcharger. Decker looked up through his windshield and saw the SUV parked just a few feet away.

• • •

Terry looked up Anna Preston's address in his Thomas Guide book and jotted down directions in one of the slim reporter's notebooks he still carried. It was probably unnecessary since the route wasn't complicated, and he'd probably remember. But he had found in his career as a reporter that writing things down helped cement them in his memory.

He took the 101 South and exited at Pleasant Valley and Santa Rosa Roads. He took a left onto Santa Rosa and drove about a mile before taking another left on Via Latina Drive, which brought him into the Mission Oaks neighborhood on the east side of Camarillo, where Preston now lived. It was an upper-middle-class area, the houses on the street were large and new, and parked along the curbs Terry observed the trucks and vans of those who made a living mowing the lawns, maintaining the pools, and cleaning the houses of the people who lived in those houses. Parking his Buick here would probably knock $5,000 off the value of every house on the street.

Preston's house was a two-story stucco with a three-car garage, set back tastefully from the street by a large front yard landscaped with rose bushes and palm trees. Terry stopped his Buick in front and hopped out, leaving the windows down. He walked up the path and knocked on the old-fashioned looking oak door.

A tall, slender woman who looked to be in her late 20s answered the door not quite a minute after Terry knocked on it. She was wearing spandex workout clothes, and her hair was tied back, a sweatband circling her head. She looked mildly surprised to have someone knocking on her door.

"I'm sorry, we don't get many salesmen around here," she said. "Whatever you're selling, I'm probably not interested." The door started swinging closed.

"Anna Preston?" Terry asked.

"Yes?" she said, a question on her face.

"Mrs. Preston, my name is Terry Cahill, and I'm not here to sell you anything. I'm a reporter, and I'm investigating a story regarding Danielle Winfield's death seven years ago. I was hoping you'd be willing to answer some questions for me."

Her face changed, and Terry could tell that she was remembering her roommate, whom she probably hadn't thought of in years.

"Would you be willing to talk to me, Mrs. Preston?" Terry continued. She broke out of her memory.

"Yes," she said. "Yes, of course. Please, come in." She opened the door all the way and Terry stepped inside the entry hallway of the house. She led him toward the back of the house and sat down at a table in a breakfast nook to the side of the kitchen. She motioned for Terry to have a seat there as well.

"I'm afraid I don't have any coffee left, Mr. Cahill," she said. "I have orange juice, or water, if you'd prefer."

"I'm fine, thank you, Mrs. Preston. Thank you for talking to me."

"Please, call me Anna."

"Thanks, Anna. Please call me Terry."

"So, what can I tell you about Danielle, Terry? I'm afraid I don't know much. I wasn't with her when she died. The police said it was an accident."

"I'm not sure exactly what I'm looking for," he said. "But I wanted to talk to you, since you were up there with her the week it happened. Can you start by telling me what she was like?"

"Fun," she said. "She was a free spirit, you know? She really enjoyed her life, loved what she did, loved the people around her. She just seemed to make everyone around her feel good. She made everything fun. I always kinda looked up to her. Like a role model, I guess. She was a few years older than me. I wanted to be like her."

"How did you meet her?"

"I worked in a little shop by the beach, sold bikinis, surfboards, skater stuff. She was one of our regular customers. I think the owner of the store had a minor sponsorship deal with her. It was nothing much, just a discount on things if she plugged our store here and there. Anyway, I worked the register, and she was looking for a roommate. I was still a teenager, just barely out of high school, and I wanted to get out of my parents' house pretty bad. She asked if I wanted to move in, and I jumped at it."

"How long did you live together?"

"Almost two years. We had a cool pad. Venice wasn't the best neighborhood back in those days, you know? But I felt safe enough at home there. And it was cheap, and it was close to the beach, and we could walk to this place to get breakfast burritos ..." she trailed off, back in a world of her own memories.

"It was good," she continued. "I'm sorry to carry on. I just really loved that time in my life. I was young, I was free, I was learning how to be an adult and live life on my own, but I didn't have to do it alone. She was my best friend. I miss her."

"I'm sorry, Anna. I know this must be difficult for you."

"I just feel bad because it's been so long since I've thought of her. I guess I tried to block it out, you know? My life is so different now. And in a lot of ways most people would probably think it's better. But when I think about back then, I miss it. I miss it so much. There wasn't a lot of money, and we ate way too much junk food, drank too much cheap beer. But we were free, and we had our whole lives ahead of us, and I miss that."

"What about the trip up to Carpinteria? You went up there with her. What can you tell me about that?"

"Oh, god. It was the summer olympics. Los Angeles was a freakin' zoo. Like, way worse than usual. Tourists just everywhere, you know? They were all over the beaches, Venice, Santa Monica. We even tried Malibu, to get away, but they were there, too. You couldn't find a place to lay your towel, or a seat at any bar.

"It was Danielle's idea to go up the coast. She booked us the motel room up in Carpinteria, and when I got home from work that day she just said 'C'mon, we're getting out of here for a while. We got in the car and went up the coast."

"What happened when you were up there?"

"The first night, nothing happened. We were both pretty wiped out from the drive up there, and it was kinda late by the time we checked in and unpacked and everything. We ate candy bars for dinner and watched MTV in our room. It was kind of a treat. We didn't have cable TV at our place.

"The next day we tried surfing at Carpinteria beach, but the waves weren't happening so we mostly just sunbathed. That night we went out. We went to a local dive bar up there, close to the motel. I remember we walked to it."

"Do you remember the name of the place?" Terry asked.

"Shakey's Tavern?"

"Shakey's? You mean like the pizza place?"

"Something like that. I don't think it was Shakey's exactly, but something that sounded like that. It was close to our motel, so it would've been close to the freeway, too."

"And what happened there?" Terry sensed that the story was going somewhere, and he wanted to keep her on it.

"Most of the night was fun. We drank margaritas and talked with the locals and had some nachos. They were good nachos, I remember. It was nice, right up until just before we left."

"What happened at the end of the night."

"There was this guy there. We had been talking to him along with some of the others at first, but then he started getting creepy. He was really hitting on Danielle. At first she flirted back a little, but when it became clear that he meant it she started backing away, trying to redirect the conversation, you know? But this guy wasn't having it. He kept on her, trying to get her to come home with him. She tried to let him down easy, but eventually she had to shoot him down hard.

"So this guy, he didn't like that. I mean, she really humiliated him, in front of his friends, I think. And then he started getting scary. He was a big guy, you know? And he was getting really aggressive. He tried grabbing her by the arm and stuff. She pulled away, but he kept grabbing at her."

"What stopped him?"

"The bartender. He'd seen what was going on, and I kept wondering if anyone was going to do anything about this guy. I caught the bartender's eyes, and thankfully he came over. He said, 'That's enough, Jon-Jon. It's time for you to leave.' And he didn't want to go, started giving the bartender a hard time, but the bartender said he wasn't kidding, and that even if he stayed around he wouldn't be getting any more free drinks, or something like that."

On hearing the name Jon-Jon, Terry had a flash of memory to the phone call with Brad Keener outside the Ventura library. *"They killed her. Jon-Jon did it ..."*

"Jon-Jon?" Terry asked. "Is that the name you remember?"

"Yeah, Jon-Jon. I remember thinking then that it was weird, because it sounded like something you'd call a little kid, but he was this huge, hairy man."

"Hairy?" Terry asked, now remembering Dave Sims's description of one of the assailants on the beach.

"Yeah, he was covered in body hair. Like a carpet. He was wearing one of those tank tops, and he had hair all over his shoulders, almost all the way up to his neck. It was gross."

"OK, so what happened after the bartender talked to Jon-Jon?"

"Well, he left, but he had killed the mood for that night, so we tabbed out and left a few minutes later. Besides, I was starting to feel pretty woozy. I was young, and didn't have a whole ton of experience drinking, but I don't remember drinking that much that night. And I don't remember getting back to the motel room, either. I remember leaving the bar, starting to walk back to the room, and then it's like nothing until I woke up the next morning."

Anna started crying, and Terry looked for a tissue to hand to her.

"And I didn't wake up until the police were pounding on the door to tell me that she was dead. I was supposed to go to the beach with her that morning, but I didn't wake up. We were going to drive down to Rincon and surf together. And I always thought ..." her voice hitched.

"I always thought that if I'd been with her, I could have saved her. I could have kept her from drowning if I'd been there. I always felt like it was partly my fault that she died."

"Rohypnol," Terry said without thinking.

"Excuse me?" Preston said.

"I'm sorry, Anna. Just thinking out loud. It sounds to me like you may have been drugged that night. Have you ever heard of Rohypnol?"

"No, what is it?"

"It's a prescription sedative, a sleeping pill. When mixed with alcohol it can have effects similar to what you described from that night. Intense intoxication, passing out, and memory loss. Some guys use it to rape women. They'll slip it into one of their drinks, and take advantage of them when the drug takes effect."

"But he was trying to get with Danielle, not me."

"He could've been trying to get you out of the way. Or he could've mistaken your drink for hers. Or it might have been one of his friends who drugged you. And without a test from that night, or around then, it's just speculation. But I've written about that kind of thing before, and your story sounds an awful lot like the victims' stories I've written."

Terry saw the realization hit her.

"I don't think it was your fault at all," he said. "Even if you had been there it still could have happened. But I don't think it's your fault you didn't wake up that morning. I think you were a victim too. I think you were drugged."

"What do you mean, 'a victim too?'"

"I don't think Danielle Winfield's death was an accident. I believe she was murdered by this Jon-Jon guy."

"Do you have any proof of that?" she asked.

"I may have something, if you are willing to help me again. I want to come back by sometime in the next couple of days with some pictures. Will you look at them and see if you can identify Jon-Jon for me?"

"Yes."

"Thank you, Anna." Terry pulled out his wallet and handed her one of his old business cards with every contact except his pager number scratched out. "I don't work there anymore," he explained. "I'm freelance.

But the pager number is still good. Please call that number if you think of anything else between now and then."

Terry's head was buzzing with what he'd just learned on the drive back up to Ventura. He was tempted to stop by Sims's house in Somis on the way, but decided against it. He wanted to get a picture of Jon-Jon and show it to both of them. If he could tie Jon-Jon to both the Capriani assault and a murder, he'd have one hell of a story.

27

Checking In

Terry had some phone calls to make. He needed to share what he'd learned talking to Anna. He parked in the marina lot and walked over to the Beam Reach. The bar was open, but Wendy wasn't there. He went back to her office behind the kitchen to use the phone. The first call was to Sheriff Baker, who kept it brief and told Terry to check back in when he had a positive ID on Jon-Jon, if he could get one. So far, the story wasn't leading to a suspect in Ventura County or a crime committed there.

The next call he made was to Vin Capriani.

"You got something for me, kid?" Vin asked.

Terry told him most of what he'd told the sheriff.

"OK," Vin said. "But why do I give a fuck about some surfer chick who was killed seven years ago? I mean, it's a sad story, but what's it got to do with my Brandon?"

"Because if it's the same guy who attacked your son, and it sounds like it is, he could end up getting the gas chamber for this. I thought you'd like to know that the legal stakes for this fucker had just gone up considerably."

"You mean I ain't gotta kill him, the state'll do it for me, is that what you're saying?"

"You might even get to watch," Terry said.

Vin laughed at the idea. "I don't ever walk into a prison voluntarily. But I might make an exception for that. Keep up the good work, kid. Let me know as soon as you know more, all right?"

"Sure thing, Vin."

Terry pressed the phone's hook switch and let it back up to call Detective Decker. He told his story a third time to the detective up in Santa Barbara.

"So, what do you think it all means, Cahill?" Decker asked.

"You remember the page I got, when I talked to who I'm pretty sure was Brad Keener? Well, one of the things he said was, 'They killed her. Jon-Jon did it.' Now I talk to Winfield's former roommate, who was with her the night before, and she says the guy trying to take Winfield home that night was called Jon-Jon by the bartender. And her description of Jon-Jon matches the description I got from a witness to another violent incident involving surfers visiting Rincon Point. It's gotta be connected."

Decker tended to agree. He was thinking back to the day that put him on this case, walking into St. Francis Hospital on a suspicious death call.

"From the description, Jon-Jon sounds like it could be Jonathan Abernathy. Local surfer, and from what I've learned, all-around douchebag."

The name sounded familiar to Terry, but he couldn't immediately place why.

"You got an address or some way I can get ahold of this Abernathy guy? I'd like to talk to him."

"Try a ouija board," Decker said.

"He's dead?"

"Shark chewed his leg off while he was surfing Rincon about a week ago. He died in the hospital."

Terry suddenly remembered the newspaper stories he'd read about the shark attacks, and groaned.

"Now, if you tell anyone one else this, I'll have your ass in jail on an obstruction charge," Decker said. "But between you and me, I'm investigating Abernathy's death as a murder."

"Murder?"

"Yeah, murder. The medical examiner determined that Abernathy was smothered in his sleep. Until you came up with this Winfield connection, I had no motive, other than Abernathy being a general shitbag, to point me toward a suspect. Now I've got a few directions to go. Only reason I'm telling you this much."

"Can you get me a picture of Abernathy? Something for a witness to identify?"

"We never busted him for anything, so it's not like we've got a mugshot or anything. All we have are the autopsy photos, and I'm not giving you those. They'll make your witnesses puke. Try the newspaper. They ran an obit on him, had some photos."

"So what about the bar?" Terry continued. "Do you know of any place up in Carpinteria named something like Shakey's Tavern?"

"Shockley's Tavern," Decker replied. "And Brad Keener is one of the owners of the joint, which happens to be a four-block walk from the payphone on 501 Linden. And it's only a block away from a Best Western."

Terry was stunned by the way the connections were lining up.

"That's gotta be the place," Terry said. "I want to talk to Keener again. See if he was working the night Winfield was there."

"A lot of people want to talk to Keener right now," Decker said. "I'm looking for him, myself. The Coast Guard found his boat with nobody on it, drifting out on the Pacific off the coast near Carpinteria. He didn't show up for work today, and it doesn't look like anyone's home at his place, either. His car is parked up at the harbor. I gotta tell you, I don't think he'll be found still breathing."

"What the fuck?" Terry said.

"My thoughts exactly," the detective replied.

"OK, before you go, detective, there's one more angle you may want to try out."

"What's that?"

"Look into reports about Shockley's Tavern. Specifically, see if there's an unusual number of women reporting being drugged there."

"Roofies?"

"That'd be my guess."

"All right, I'll check it out if I have time."

28

Directions

Detective Rick Decker of the Santa Barbara Sheriff's Office Detective Bureau, Crimes Against Persons division, was sitting at home in front of a muted TV and thinking about the murders he was investigating. He had a few different ways he could run with this, but he knew only one would lead to the truth. No matter which way he chose, the murder, as he now thought of it, of Danielle Winfield was probably involved.

He dismissed the idea of Ventura mobster Vin Capriani being behind the recent murders for a few reasons. First, Capriani almost certainly didn't know the identity of his son's assailant — most likely Jonathan Abernathy — before Jon-Jon got snuffed. But beyond that, if Capriani had killed Jon-Jon, what would his motive be for killing the Keener brothers? Had they been on the beach the day Capriani's son was attacked?

It was probably worth looking into, but it didn't feel right to Decker. The murders had the feel of a criminal conspiracy coming apart at the seams, and Decker believed that when the murders were solved the motivation behind them would have more to do with keeping people quiet than revenge. The person behind them went to some lengths to disguise the deaths as something other than murders, which would be rare in mob revenge killings. The mob either made a statement with their killings, shooting their victims in public, or they disappeared them with no trace left behind.

He discounted the idea of Anna Preston's involvement for similar reasons. It was reasonable to believe that Preston had thought Winfield's death was accidental for all these years. Besides, the video footage from the hospital strongly suggested that the killer was male. It was possible Preston could have done it with an accomplice, but Decker considered it so unlikely as to not be worth pursuing.

Decker had searched Abernathy's home after his death. There were a few things of interest inside, one of them being an illegal set of brass knuckles, another being a stack of Polaroid photos depicting scenes of sexual activity, which Decker wrote off as typical homemade porn.

There was also a foil package containing round white tablets in the medicine cabinet. They could have been mistaken for over-the-counter cold medication, or something else innocuous, but Decker had recognized them as Rohypnol.

Rohypnol, or "roofies," or "Mexican Quaaludes," among other street names, were abused in a number of ways. Some users of uppers took them to come down from a high, to allow them to sleep after a binge. Others mixed them with alcohol or marijuana for a near-comatose state of intoxication. And some guys used them to take advantage of women sexually. Something told Decker that this last use wouldn't be out of character for Abernathy, and that the pills and the pictures he'd found in his two-bedroom bungalow were connected.

But if Abernathy had been killed by an angry boyfriend of a victim, or something along those lines, why kill Scott Keener and make his brother disappear?

He kept looking for what tied all three victims together. The Keener brothers had both talked to that reporter Cahill from Ventura. The elder Keener had mentioned a murder, and tied Jon-Jon to it. The way things were shaping up, it sounded like the murder had been real, and Abernathy looked good for it. But that couldn't be all, could it?

Silence Abernathy, the killer. Keeps him from confessing, maybe implicating others in that crime. Then silence anybody else who might be willing to talk about it? Sounds likely enough.

...

Terry was up early, making a mondo batch of his chili in the kitchen of the Beam Reach before the bar opened. Wendy had sold out of the first small batch quickly, selling it by the mug with a couple of packages of oyster crackers, and she wanted the next batch to be big enough to last at least through the lunch hour. He was just adding some wine and stirring the pot when his pager went off. It was Desmond. He went back to the office to use the phone and return his father-in-law's call.

"Hey, Des. What can I do for you?"

"Hi, Terry. Actually, I do have a favor to ask of you."

"Fire away."

"You remember you said that you would be willing to accompany Mallory to therapy sessions, if she were to seek help?"

"Yeah, I remember. Just tell me when and where, and I'll meet her there."

"Well, I'm afraid I need to ask a little more than that."

Terry felt he wasn't going to like what was coming next.

"Uh, OK. What do you need?"

"We booked her a session with a therapist up here, great reputation. I think it will really help her. The thing is, she doesn't want to drive up here by herself. Her mom offered to come down and pick her up, but she says if you're going anyway she wants to ride with you."

"Ah, man." Terry thought about it for a moment. "I'm not sure that's such a swell idea. I mean, I'm willing to talk with her, but I'd prefer it to be in a supervised environment. I'm not sure we should be alone together."

"I understand your reservations, but she doesn't seem willing to come up any other way. Can you help us out here?"

"Do you really think it'll be good for her? I mean, do you think riding up to Santa Barbara and back with me won't undo whatever good is done in therapy?"

"I believe it is worth trying. That's the best I can do."

"OK. I'll do it. We can see how it goes this time. When and where is the appointment?"

Desmond gave him an address on State Street south of the 101, along with a suite number, and said the appointment was for 11 a.m. That meant he'd have to plan on picking his soon-to-be ex up no later than 10 a.m. if they were going to be there on time.

"All right. Thanks, Desmond. I'll get her there."

"No, thank you, Terry. I know it's an imposition."

Terry hung up the phone and sat in the worn leather office chair behind Wendy's desk for a moment, feeling like he'd just been run over by a medium-sized truck. It was just like Mallory to insist on getting her own way. And per usual, it looked like she was going to get it.

Still, Terry knew there was no use getting angry about it. His initial impulse when parting with her had been to make a clean and complete break with her, to basically vanish from her life. And that impulse had been inspired by the knowledge that any remaining tie to her would be something she could exploit, in ways much like this.

But he'd later realized that making that break with her would also hurt other people he cared about. He knew he'd had a choice to make, and either way he went had uncomfortable consequences attached.

He decided to get over it and go back to stirring his chili. He had other things to do today.

...

When he was done making the chili at the Beam Reach, Terry stopped back by *Easy Goer* for a quick change of clothes, then got in his Buick and headed for the E. P. Foster Library across the 101 in Downtown Ventura. He felt like there was something he was missing about this story he was chasing, and for some reason he couldn't place he decided there might be something less than random about the recent spate of shark attacks at Rincon.

While the stories he wanted to read were still relatively new, and would not be on microfiche yet, he reasoned that he should know the deeper history of sharks approaching near the beaches in the area. He wanted a historical perspective, because while he suspected the the incidents were an aberration, he wouldn't really know unless he did the research.

He referred to the list of articles on shark attacks Herb had given him, and searched for stories going back from the 1920s to the present day that involved sharks and the area beaches. He was rewarded with a volume of stories he couldn't possibly read in just a couple of hours, so he picked three or four that looked promising from each decade and went back to the microfiche readers to scan them.

The stories were pretty much what he expected; shark attacks were exceedingly rare on Southern California beaches, although sightings were not terribly uncommon. There was one story he found interesting, though. It was from 1934, and told the tale of a fishing boat that had sunk just off the coast near Oxnard, coming back after a successful voyage. There had been an explosion onboard, and the sunken boat with its holds full of fish attracted sharks for about a week. The state had to close the beaches during that time.

He brought the microfiche slides back to the desk and asked a librarian for the recent periodical back issues, specifically the last week's worth of local newspapers from Ventura and Santa Barbara Counties. What he found was a few stories in the local papers that pretty much went over the same ground as the stories he'd read before. One of the stories that caught his eye was an obituary for Jonathan Abernathy printed in the *Santa Barbara Spyglass*.

Terry looked at the picture accompanying the article and got his first look at Abernathy. *So that's Jon-Jon*, he thought. He was shown standing on a beach next to a surfboard planted tail-first in the sand, grinning for the camera, his aloha shirt unbuttoned to reveal a chest almost black with hair. *Reminds me of Bluto from the old Popeye comics.*

The obituary portrayed Abernathy as a fun-loving guy, beloved by his community and dearly missed by all. It made no mention of foul play, only noting that Abernathy had died at St. Francis Hospital in Santa Barbara following his being bitten by a shark while surfing.

Terry had a hunch and checked the date of the *Spyglass* with the Abernathy obit, then pulled up the *Monitor* from the same day. He paged through the sections, and sure enough, the *Monitor* had run a blurb about Abernathy's death as well. The *Monitor's* story used a different photo from his obit in the *Spyglass*. Terry checked the byline and found that it was a wire story. That could mean that there were multiple images, and that the *Monitor* had run the one that best fit in the space allowed.

He returned the papers to the librarian and left the library.

29

Back Rooms

Deputy Kirkham was meeting with Dewey Michaels again. This time after hours, in a booth in the private dining room in the back of Zadini's, an Italian restaurant on West Cabrillo Boulevard across from the Santa Barbara Harbor. It was a dimly lit space, complete with the requisite wood paneled walls and red leather booths. The two men had the room to themselves, and talked over heaping plates of pasta that were being tragically ignored.

"The Coasties found Brad's boat yesterday," Kirkham said, reaching for his glass of red. "No sign of life, on the boat or anywhere near it."

"What the fuck is going on here, Kerry?" Michaels asked, picking at his linguine half-heartedly. "Scotty's killed himself? Now Brad's disappeared?"

"Look, I don't want to panic you, man."

"But?" Dewey asked, expecting to be panicked.

"But, you know that kid Jon-Jon knocked out a couple of weeks ago? The one who hit his head on the rocks?"

"Yeah? He's not dead, is he?"

"Not yet. He's in a coma at VC Med. His name is Brandon Capriani."

Michaels put down his fork and looked at the deputy.

"You mean?"

"Yeah, his dad. Vin Capriani."

"Oh, good Christ, that's just what we need. You think the mob is knocking us off, one-by-one like?"

"I don't know. But what do you think a mob boss would do if we put his son in a coma?"

"Actually, I'd expect him to take us all out at once. Guns blazing, you know?"

"You've seen too many movies. That's not how a guy like Vin operates. The Ventura arm of the Outfit has always kept a low profile, ever since the rum-running days. They're in business to make money, not attract attention. I think this is exactly the kind of thing he would do."

"So you think it's him? How the hell do we ..."

"I didn't say that, exactly," Kirkham said, cutting Michaels off. "It could be him. It could be someone else. There was a reporter sniffing around it too. At least he said he was a reporter. He and a bunch of hard-asses beat the shit out of Scotty and Billy and a couple of the other guys last week. Scotty was talking to him."

"Could be Capriani's guys."

"Could be. Or it could be someone else with a reason. Dewey, I wasn't kidding about Jon-Jon. He pissed a lot of people off. Besides all the shit at the beach, there was the scam he was pulling at Shockley's, probably other bars too. Could be an angry boyfriend, or even a father, come to collect." He stuffed a meatball in his mouth before continuing.

"And then there's what happened seven years ago," Kirkham said, looking Michaels in the eye.

Dewey Michaels winced at the mention of the killing of Danielle Winfield. "Don't remind me," he said. He wasn't even pretending to eat anymore. He drained his gin and tonic and immediately wished for another.

"But if it's a father or whatever, or it's about the surfer girl he killed all those years ago, why kill Scotty and Brad?"

"Could be a few reasons. Could be whoever's doing it sees us as all being part of the same crime. We did cover up the thing with the surfer girl, if it's about her. Or, maybe Scotty really just offed himself. Maybe his brother couldn't take it and went out on his boat late the other night. Maybe he jumped, or maybe something happened, an accident, rogue wave, something like that. Maybe we'll never know."

"Yeah," Michaels. "Or maybe we find out when one of Vin's guys puts a bullet between our eyes."

"Look, I don't want you to get panicked over this. Like I said, it could be coincidence. It could be nothing, really. But whatever it is, loosing our cool will just make it worse, OK? We've gotta stay calm, deal with things as we figure 'em out."

"I have some contacts that could put me in touch with Capriani. Maybe we should put word out, request a meeting. We could offer something, try to make amends."

"That is, look, that's a really bad idea, OK? We don't know it's Vin, and if it's not, and he doesn't know anything about us, we've just painted a bright red target on all our asses. Just sit tight, and keep a low profile for a little while. I'll keep you informed, and we'll decide what to do when we know what's going on."

"It doesn't feel like a coincidence," Michaels. "Three of us dead in a week, maybe four, and these fucking sharks literally eating us alive." He reached for his empty G&T. "It feels like God is punishing us."

• • •

Twenty-eight miles south, Terry Cahill was meeting with Sheriff Baker in Wendy's office in the back of the Beam Reach. Wendy came in with three beers, set two of them on the desk, and plopped down on the couch she sometimes crashed on when she didn't feel like walking back to *Clara* for the night.

Terry was sitting behind the desk, and Tim was in one of the chairs on the other side. Terry was catching the sheriff up on what he'd learned so far, and the hunches he wanted to play.

"So, I need to get pictures of these guys, especially Jon-Jon, and see if Sims or Preston recognize them," Terry said.

"You need more than just that," Tim said. "The way we do it, when we want a witness to ID someone, is we bring 'em a six-pack."

"I don't see how getting 'em drunk will help, but if you gotta do that bring 'em in here," Wendy piped in from the couch.

"Not beer," Tim said. "We bring in six pictures. Five cops, usually, and the suspect. Show the witness all the pics and ask which one. If we're saying, 'Identify this person,' and then we only show them that one person, it could get thrown out in court. It's like we told them to do it, tainted the memory. And then that witness's entire testimony could become inadmissible."

"OK, I guess we don't want that," Terry said. "Can you get me some pics of cops who fit the description?"

"I can probably make that happen, yeah. And I should probably go down there too, be there for the ID, make sure we do it right."

"So I take it you won't be taking the early shift tomorrow, huh, Terry?" Wendy asked.

"Ah, shit, I can't do it tomorrow. I've gotta pick up Mal in the morning and drive her up to Santa Barbara for an appointment with her therapist. I almost forgot about it. Got no idea how long it'll take, but I'd better plan for it being the whole day."

"She can't drive her own ass up there?" Wendy asked.

"She won't," Terry replied. "Don't worry, I'll come in early to make a batch of chili before I go."

It's pretty important to get this," Tim said.

"It's OK. I'll get Jody in here," Wendy said.

"I can work the afternoon shift, after I take Mal and before we talk to Sims and Preston," Terry offered. "Tim, I can make the trip down to Camarillo tomorrow evening if that works for you."

"Give me a call before you head down there," Tim said. "I'll meet you out there."

30

Santa Barbara

Detective Decker was at home when Dr. Kreutz called. He had asked her to not call him at the office. He wasn't willing to let anyone overhear the conversation he expected to have. He didn't have a concrete reason for it. Just an intuition that was talking a bit louder than usual.

"Morning, doc," he said into the receiver.

"Good morning, detective," she said. "I've taken a look at Danielle Winfield's tox screen from the autopsy. I think there's something interesting there."

Decker waited for the doctor to continue.

"There were trace amounts of Flunitrazepam in her system," she said. "Not enough to account for a full dose. In fact, it was barely even there. But it was there."

"Roofies," Decker said.

"Yes. What's more, there were no traces of any other drugs in her system, illicit or otherwise. She had been metabolizing alcohol, but no evidence of, say, marijuana abuse or anything similar, nor was there evidence of long-term use of Flunitrazepam as there would be had it been prescribed to her."

"What does that tell you, doc?"

"It suggests that she was drugged. She did not show signs of being a recreational drug user, so it's unlikely that she chose to abuse

Flunitrazepam, and she also did not show signs of using it legally as a prescribed sedative. The most reasonable conclusion is that somebody drugged her with it at some point within the last couple of days before her death."

"You said it was trace amounts, not enough to account for a full dosage. How can you tell? I mean, could it be a full dose from longer ago and she just metabolized most of it before dying?"

"I don't consider that the most likely scenario. Flunitrazepam has an elimination half-life ranging from around 12 hours to a day. That means it is cleared of the system relatively quickly, and from what you told me of the case she wouldn't have been exposed to it until the night before her death. Of course, I'd need a hair sample to be sure, but going on what I've got here, I think I've given you the most probable explanation."

"Do you think the dose she got was enough to cause impairment?"

"I can't say. She definitely had alcohol in her system, and that complicates things. And everyone reacts differently to drugs. I can't even say for sure what the dosage was, only that it was probably small. It's possible she was impaired. It's also possible that she didn't feel a thing from it."

"OK, thank you, doc. You've been very helpful."

•••

Terry dragged himself out of his bunk on *Easy Goer* at an hour to which he was no longer accustomed, all so he could make a batch of chili for Wendy before driving Mallory to her therapy session all the way up in Santa Barbara. He skipped his morning routine of having tea in the cockpit of the boat and watching the marine layer thin out. He hoped Charlie the dock cat, who had been visiting regularly, wouldn't mind too much.

The Beam Reach was deserted at this hour, and he used his key to let himself in. Terry liked cooking when no one else was around to get in the way. He was sure that Wendy could figure out his recipe if she wanted to, but still felt that making the chili himself offered some safeguard. He fried up a couple of extra slices of bacon for himself to munch on so the smell of the food cooking wouldn't drive him totally mad with hunger.

As soon as the batch was done cooking, he covered the vat and placed it in the refrigerator to cool off. His recommendation to Wendy was to have the kitchen heat up individual orders as they came in instead of leaving the chili on the stove all day, which could cause it to burn. He hung up his apron and walked back to *Easy Goer* to pick up his shower bag and get ready for the rest of his day.

He pulled up to the curb in front of his former house on McKinley Drive a little early. Checking his Timex, he decided to go knock on the door and see how late Mallory planned to be, and see if he could maybe speed things along. Mallory answered in a thick, fuzzy pink bathrobe. Terry stood back far enough from the doorway to be out of range of any attempt at a hug.

"Hi," she said. "It's good to see you. I'm still getting ready. Come on in. I'll only be a few more minutes."

Terry knew her definition of "a few more minutes" could stretch out to two hours or longer.

"Ah, thanks," he said. "I'll just wait out in the car." It might not help to expedite the process, he knew, but he didn't want to set foot in that house again if he could help it.

"You sure?" she asked, a sad expression growing on her face. "I could get you some coffee or something."

"No, thank you. Probably shouldn't have any more coffee today. Besides, it's nice outside. I'll be here when you're ready."

He went back to his car and sat down on the plush bench seat. He'd had the windows open for the drive over, but knew he'd be rolling those up and running the air for Mallory on the drive to Santa Barbara. It was nice to just sit and enjoy the breeze blowing through the hardtop on the warm summer morning. To his mild surprise, Mallory came out of the house less than half an hour later. They were going to be late, but not as late as he'd anticipated.

She walked down the driveway looking confused. She didn't see Terry. Then she noticed the ratty old Buick parked at the curb, Terry waving at her from behind the steering wheel, and her face fell into an expression of shock. Or was it disgust? Some combination of the two, probably.

"Oh, no," she said, leaning through the passenger side window. "No, Terry, forget it. you're not driving me to Santa Barbara in this piece of shit."

"OK, suit yourself," Terry said. "Your father said you needed a ride, and I'm willing to drive you there. But this is the only car I've got."

"Please, Terry, please, can you just drive me up there in my BMW? I don't see why we have to take this car."

"I hate driving that car, Mal. It breaks down all the time, and it smells like old crayons."

"What about your truck? It's still here. We could go in that."

"I don't want to argue about it. This is the car I have. If you want a ride up with me, that's fine. But if I'm driving, I'm driving my own car. If you want to drive, you can take your car, or your truck, or whatever else you want."

"But it's not *safe*," she wailed. "And it looks like something a poor person would drive."

"Well, I am a poor person. I guess it's appropriate. But I understand your concern. Maybe you should just take your car. It's a nice day. Should be a lovely drive up the coast. You could put the top down." He reached over to the ignition and started the Buick's absurdly large engine. Her arm shot out for the passenger door handle as he was grabbing the column-mounted shifter to put the car in Drive.

"No, wait," she said. "Let me go with you." She opened the door and slid in. "I don't know why you've got to be so difficult about it." She buckled her lap belt as he pulled away from the curb, Terry noticed with amusement. Mallory didn't usually like to wear a seatbelt.

He rolled up the windows without her asking, and turned on the AC so the car wouldn't get uncomfortable. Chet Atkins was playing softly on the tape deck.

"That reminds me," she said. "I've got that case of your old cassettes out of your truck." Terry didn't think of the Toyota in her garage as 'his,' but let that go. "I've been listening to them. I used to wonder why you liked that corny old shitkicker music, but I think I get it now."

"You may want to listen to something a little more uplifting. I don't know that this stuff is doing you any good."

"I like it because it reminds me of you. Sometimes it's almost like you're still around. I even bought a guitar. I thought I'd learn to play it."

"Well, who knows. Maybe someday I'll be listening to one of your tapes driving around."

"Even if the songs are about you?"

"Hmm, yeah. Maybe not."

She reached across the bench seat for his hand and held it in hers. He wanted to pull away, but he didn't want to set her off on a crying jag. So he let her hold his hand. They made small talk in fits and starts, punctuated by long stretches of the Chet Atkins tape, until they finally arrived at the therapist's office.

• • •

It was past noon when Mallory was finished with her first session with the therapist. Terry had spent the time in the waiting room, after being briefly introduced. He had bided the time absent-mindedly browsing the out-of-date magazines left out on a table while thinking about the story he was working on. That's how he thought of it: Not a case, but a story, as if he were still reporting.

Mallory came out of the therapist's office looking considerably sunnier than she had walking in.

"Thanks for being here for me, Terry," she said. "It means a lot to me."

"I wasn't really in there, you know."

"I know. But just knowing you're out here for me, that you're taking me home, it means a lot that you would do this for me. I just want you to know that."

"Ah, you're welcome, Mal. I'm glad you seem to be feeling better."

"He said after a couple more sessions he'd like to bring you in, if you're OK with it, get your perspective on things."

"Just let me know. I'll try to fit it in."

"You're a dear," she said, and swept in and kissed him on the cheek. "And to help make up for all the shit I put you through this morning, let me buy you lunch. Are you hungry?"

He was. And while he wasn't thrilled about the idea of a lunch date with the woman he was trying to divorce, the idea of driving all the way back to Ventura on an empty stomach appealed to him less.

"I know a great little Italian place around the corner on Cabrillo, by the harbor. My parents used to take me there when I was a kid."

"That sounds nice."

It was nice. Terry found the food at Zadini's exceptional. He had the chicken parmesan, and, in deference to Mallory, let her change his order for a Miller Lite to a bottle of Peroni. They were almost done with their late lunch, and Terry was finishing off his beer when an agitated man emerged from the back of the restaurant with a sheriff's deputy behind him.

Terry looked over, as did a few of the other patrons, and recognized the man as Dewey Michaels. He had never met Michaels in person, but he knew his face from the newspaper articles he'd read about him. The deputy's name tag said 'Kirkham,' and that rang bells for Terry as well, although he couldn't quite place them. He made a mental note of the incident and reminded himself to check out the name Kirkham later.

"Look, I'll talk to some people in Ventura about it, OK?" Deputy Kirkham was saying. It looked like he was trying to placate Michaels.

"I want this cleared up ..." Michaels said as the two men left through the front door.

Mallory noticed the diversion of his attention from her, and snapped him out of it.

"Is something wrong?" she asked.

"Ah, no. Just thought I saw someone I knew."

• • •

Terry checked his reporter's notebook as soon as he'd dropped Mallory back off at her home in Ventura. He was flipping through the pages looking for the name 'Kirkham.' Eventually he found it, in reference to the story about Danielle Winfield's death. He pulled away from the curb on McKinley Drive and set course for the Beam Reach for his afternoon shift. He was running late, but there were still some things he wanted to check out.

31

Confirmation

Terry was in Wendy's office at the Beam Reach. There were three things on his to-do list. He wanted to see the police report from the Winfield incident at Rincon. He also wanted to talk to both Sims and Anna. If Sims could identify Jon-Jon from the beach that day, or if Anna could identify him from the bar the night before Winfield's death, that would be something worth following up. That meant Terry would need to obtain some photographs of the Santa Barbara Boys before talking to them. And the quickest way to get those would be through Herb.

"Already want to buy me lunch again?" Herb said.

"I was hoping you could help me out with some backissues." Terry pulled his notebook out and flipped to the notes he'd taken at the library. He gave Herb the dates and the page numbers for the articles that featured pictures of the Santa Barbara Boys.

"What do you need them for?" Herb asked.

"I'm writing up a story, freelance, about violence on our beaches. I need to show the pictures to a witness to see if he can identify any of them."

"Those backissues aren't supposed to leave the morgue, you know that. I don't even let reporters take them to their desks."

"I could bring them back," Terry offered.

"I might be able to do better. I can probably find the photos they used and let you take those. They'd probably never be missed."

"Thanks, Herb." Terry thought for a second. "Hey, do you think you could throw in some random images of people with these? Beach scenes, if you've got them?"

Herb hesitated to answer, but thought better of asking his friend and former colleague what he was up to.

"Yeah, I guess I could do that. How will I get them to you?"

"You know the Beam Reach, down on the Marina?"

"Burgers are all right. The rest of the food, eh, not so much?"

"That's all changed. Best chili you've ever had, I guarantee it."

"Put some of that chili on one of their burgers, and I'll be there."

"See you then." Terry hung up.

• • •

While he was waiting for Herb, and before starting his shift, Terry made another phone call, this time to Detective Rick Decker in Santa Barbara.

"If it isn't my favorite unemployed reporter," Decker said.

"Good afternoon to you too," Terry said. "I was hoping you could answer a question for me."

"I guess that depends on the question, Cahill. What do you want to know?"

"Who signed the official police report on Danelle Winfield?"

Decker considered for a moment. The information was public record, and Cahill could find it by filing the proper request. That would take time, of course, but his inclination was to let the press do their own work and not give them much of anything, public record or not. While he was thinking about it, Cahill broke in.

"Was it Deputy Kirkham?" he asked.

"Yeah, it was Kirkham. He was the responding officer."

"Was he the only officer on the scene?"

"No. He was the only officer to respond initially, but he was met by backup."

"How long did it take for the other officers to arrive?"

"That I don't know. I wasn't there. In fact, I wasn't with Santa Barbara yet when it happened."

"Is there any way to find out?"

"There might be a record from the dispatch logs, if they've been kept. Where are you going with this, Cahill?"

"Maybe nowhere," Terry said. "But I did see Deputy Kirkham leaving Zadini's with Dewey Michaels this afternoon. They were having what appeared to be an uncomfortable conversation. And Dewey Michaels, according to one of my sources, is the leader of the Santa Barbara Boys surf gang. Does that interest you?"

"Not really," Decker lied. He made a mental note to check Kirkham's activity logs to see what he put down as his lunch break for the day.

"OK, well, that's all I've got for now. I'm going to show Anna Preston some pictures this evening. I'll let you know whether we get an ID on anyone."

"Sounds good," Decker said. "Speaking of Mrs. Preston, there is something I can pass along there."

"Oh?"

"Danielle Winfield had trace amounts of Flunitrazepam in her system the morning she died. That mean anything to you?"

"Rohypnol," Terry said. "She was roofied."

"Doc says it doesn't look like a full dose."

"Maybe she didn't finish her drink," Terry suggested.

"Yeah, that could explain it."

He finished the call and hung up the phone, wondering where this left him. An idea of what had happened the night before Winfield's death was beginning to take shape in the back of his mind.

• • •

"I got the pictures for you," Herb said as he entered the Beam Reach. He was carrying a large manilla envelope, which he placed on the bar in front of Terry. Terry opened a Michelob and set it in front of Herb.

"Much appreciated, Herb."

"You didn't tell me you worked here," Herb said.

"Yeah, well, it's just part time."

"But you're working on a story?"

"Yeah, freelance. Gotta do what I can in the meantime, you know?"

"I hear that."

• • •

Terry's turn behind the bar ended at 6 p.m. He'd already phoned the sheriff during one of his breaks, and he walked out of the Reach to find Tim in a patrol car waiting in the parking lot.

"We riding together?" Terry asked.

"Might as well," Tim said. "No need for you to blow a bigger hole in the ozone layer with that yacht of yours if we're both coming back here."

"I think we should hit Sims first, since he's kind of on the way."

"We could hit him on the way there or the way back."

"Yeah, I guess it doesn't matter."

Traffic was mild for most of the drive south to Camarillo and Somis. Most of it was headed the other way, commuters trying to get home. They stayed on the 101 all the way to Lewis. On the way there, the sheriff had

Terry add the photos he got from the newspaper to a set of photos he had brought from the station.

Nobody answered the bell at the Sims house. Tim parked his patrol car on the side of the road, and both men got out to look around. Not much of the property was visible behind the fence. Terry saw an outbuilding, looked like a big shed, and could see that the doors were left open. Inside, he saw two metal cages. He didn't know what they were. They didn't look like they were kennels, or made for livestock like chickens. They were round.

"Hey, Tim, take a look at this," Terry said.

The sheriff came over to where Terry was looking through the fence.

"What do you think those are?" Terry asked, pointing at the open building.

"Lobster cages," Tim said. "Old ones. C'mon, let's go to Preston's before it gets any later. I don't think there's anything here for us."

As they were getting into the car, the breeze picked up, carrying the foul odor of decomposition with it. Both men noticed it and looked at each other.

"Jesus!" Terry exclaimed, gagging.

"Probably a dead animal around here."

"You don't think ..." Terry asked.

"You mean a body in the house? We probably wouldn't smell that all the way out here. Most likely it's roadkill, or maybe the remains of a coyote's dinner."

"What about probable cause?"

"What, to enter the property?" The sheriff thought for a moment. "Probably not enough. It's the country, and dead animals aren't that uncommon in places like this. Unless I have reason to believe that smell is a person, it doesn't hold up. Do you have reason to believe Sims or anyone in his household is in danger?"

"No, not really."

"Then it's not enough. And like I said, it's probably an animal. People smell different somehow. Worse."

They got back in the car and drove to Camarillo.

"I didn't call ahead," Terry said. "I hope she's there."

"I called, about an hour before I came and got you," Tim said. "She's expecting us."

"Oh, good."

The sheriff parked on the street in front of Anna Preston's house. The two of them walked up the long path to the front door, which was answered almost immediately by a middle-aged man wearing a golf shirt and slacks. He looked alarmed to see a uniformed police officer on his doorstep, and Terry wondered whether everyone in the household was aware of their visit.

"Can I help you?" the man asked.

"We're here to speak with Anna Preston," Sheriff Baker said. "She is expecting us."

"Well, what's this all about? Did she get a ticket or something? I mean, surely there's no reason to come here at night parking a police car in front of my house."

"Your wife is not in any kind of trouble. She is helping us out voluntarily. The rest isn't really any of your concern."

"Now wait just a minute," the man said. "You're the guys who've been coming down here upsetting my wife. I don't know what you have to talk about, but I'd prefer you talk to me instead of getting her all emotional."

"Sir, we are conducting a criminal investigation involving the death of a person, and you are not the person we need to speak to. If you attempt to prevent us from doing so, you will technically be guilty of obstruction of justice, and ..."

"It's OK, Gary," a woman's voice interrupted from inside the house. "I want to talk to them."

"Honey, you've been crying off and on since the last time you talked to them," Gary Preston said. "I don't think you should put yourself through this again."

"I *want* to," Anna Preston said to her husband, appearing in the doorway. There was steel in her eyes when she looked at him, and he backed away. "Please, come in," she said to Terry and Sheriff Baker.

"Thank you," Tim said.

The entered the house and went back to the same breakfast nook where Terry and Anna had talked before. The kitchen was the best-lit room in the house, and the sheriff was happy that she chose it without being asked.

"We have some photographs for you to look at," Terry said.

"Well, let's get to it," she said. "I've been looking forward to this, believe it or not."

"I'm sorry to have upset you, by the way," Terry said.

"You didn't," she replied. "I'm upset, yes, but not because of you. I'm upset because my friend is gone. I guess you just reminded me of how much I've missed her. But if I can do something to help her now, well, that makes me feel a little better about things."

Anna sat down at the table with Terry and the sheriff, and the sheriff opened the envelope with the pictures in it and started handing them to her. She looked at the first couple of photographs and then stopped on the third. Both men saw her eyes widen in fear as she looked at that third image. Terry glanced over. It was the image of Jonathan Abernathy standing on a beach. The picture had been blown up and cropped like a mug shot, to match the style of the other photographs in the six pack.

"That's Jon-Jon," she said, and her expression changed from fear to hate. "That's the guy Danielle got kicked out of the bar that night."

"Are you sure that's him?" the sheriff asked.

"A hundred percent," she said, looking at some of the other photos. She pulled another one out of the pile and pointed. "See this guy? He looks a lot like him, but it's not him. He's got the hair all over and he looks big, but the face isn't right." She pointed at another picture. "This one looks close too, but the nose is too big, and his shoulders are too square looking." She went back to the photo of Abernathy. "This is the guy. I'm positive."

"OK, thank you Mrs. Preston," the sheriff said. "Can you keep looking to see if you recognize any of the others?"

She went back to the stack of photos and spent several minutes looking at them before pulling another out of the pile. It was a group shot taken on the beach. She pointed at the second man from the left.

"That guy," she said. "He looks like the bartender at Shakey's."

She was pointing at Billy Newhouse.

"Actually, we've found the place is called Shockley's Tavern," Terry said. He saw recognition on her face.

"Shockley's," she said quietly. "That's it."

"And you're sure this is the bartender?" the sheriff asked.

"Not as sure as I am with the other one," she said. "But pretty sure. It was either him, or someone who looked a lot like him. And nobody else in these photos looks like him."

Both men nodded without noticing.

"OK, thank you, Mrs. Preston," the sheriff said. "Your help means a lot, and we appreciate it."

"You catch this guy and I'll be the one appreciating you," she said.

"I've been thinking about what you told me about that night, about how you blacked out at the end of the night," Terry said. "And I have been meaning to ask you if you remember any more, if anything came to you since we last talked."

"Bits and pieces," she said. "Little flashes here and there. Nothing I can really put together, though."

"What about what you were drinking?" he pressed on. "You said you were drinking margaritas that night. Were you both drinking the same thing?"

"Yeah, at first we were. We both had margaritas starting out, but then after the first couple I switched to beer. I was still a lightweight, and I didn't want to get drunk too fast."

"So when you switched to beer, Danielle kept drinking the margaritas?" Terry asked. The sheriff was watching him work, not wanting to get in the way. He had a feeling Terry was onto something.

"Yeah, she was ..." she trailed off.

"I'm just wondering," Terry said. "Is it possible that at some point in the night your drinks got mixed up? Like, you got hers and she got yours?"

"No, not mixed up. I think we traded." Terry and the sheriff could see her recalling the memory from long ago, and let her pull it out at her own pace.

"She was drinking house margaritas, but that guy who was hitting on her, that Jon-Jon guy? He heard her ordering one, but he told the bartender something like 'Don't let her drink that, upgrade her to a Cadillac,' or something like that. And Danielle didn't like it. She said it tasted funny. So I grabbed it and took a sip. It didn't taste funny to me, so I took her drink and she took my beer."

"How many of the Cadillac margaritas did you have?" Terry asked.

"I think just that one," she said. "I think those were the last drinks we had, and then things started getting ugly, and that Jon-Jon guy got kicked out, and then we left. I don't know for sure. That's around the time things start getting fuzzy for me. But I'm pretty sure we didn't drink any more after that."

Terry and the sheriff traded a knowing look.

"Do you remember what I told you I thought the last time we talked?" Terry asked. "About how you might have been drugged."

"Yes, and I told you he was after ..." her face showed that the penny had dropped. "He drugged her drink, and then I drank it," she said softly.

"And from what you've said tonight, it sounds like the bartender was in on it," Terry continued.

"Requesting the upgrade to a Cadillac," the sheriff said. "That was their code."

Terry nodded in the affirmative.

"Sounds like it," Terry said.

"So it really wasn't my fault," Anna Preston said, looking down at the table.

"It was never your fault," Terry said. "Even if you weren't drugged."

"That's not how it felt for the last seven years," she said. She was starting to cry. She looked down at the picture of Abernathy, and suddenly let out a scream of rage and slammed her fist down on the picture.

"What the hell is going on in here?" said Gary Preston, poking his head around the corner.

"Not now, Gary," Anna said tiredly. "These men have just helped me. I just needed to let that out. It's fine."

"It doesn't sound fine," he said.

"This is not your business, Mr. Preston," the sheriff said. "You need to cool it." He turned to Anna and Terry. "I think we have what we need here. Thank you, Mrs. Preston. Your help has been invaluable."

The two men got up to leave.

"Are you going to catch him," she asked. "Is this enough?"

Terry and the sheriff looked at each other. Terry took the signal and went with it.

"Anna, I don't know how to tell you this, but Jon-Jon, well, his real name was Jonathan Abernathy," he said.

"Was?" Anna said.

"He's dead," Terry said. "A shark bit his leg off while he was surfing at Rincon Point. He died in the hospital."

She just looked at him with a numb expression.

"But the bartender," Terry continued. "We think he was involved, and we will go after him. We are going to make sure he pays. And we think there may have been others involved, too."

They walked to the front door. As they were leaving, Anna stopped Terry and hugged him tight against her.

"Thank you," she said. "Thank you for helping me stop blaming myself for what happened. And thank you for caring about what happened to my friend."

Terry didn't know what to say. He just let her hug him, then walked down to Sheriff Baker's patrol car for the drive back to Ventura.

32

The Long Night

Terry was turning things over and over in his head as he rode with the sheriff back to Ventura. He knew that the conversation with Anna Preston should be the fresher memory, the one that stood out to him in starkest relief, but his mind kept going back to the visit to the Sims house. He remembered that smell from the nights he'd been woken up by the sound of someone on the dock.

"What are your plans for the rest of the night?" Terry asked his friend the sheriff.

"I'm gonna write up our encounter with Mrs. Preston, then go home and have a late dinner. Sorry, no drinks at the Reach tonight."

"That's not what I was thinking, actually."

"Oh, shit, Terry, what do you have in mind?" Tim had an idea he wouldn't like what was coming next.

He was right.

"I keep thinking about those shark attacks on Rincon," Terry said. "The more I think about them, the more I think they're connected to this thing with the Santa Barbara Boys."

Terry told the sheriff what he had in mind.

"Well, that would mean a piece of this thing is solidly on my turf," the sheriff said when Terry was done.

"So you're in?"

"Yeah, I'm in. But it's thin, and for now, at least, I want to keep this off the books."

"Good. Let's go to the Reach and get some coffee. You got a thermos in here?"

•••

"Wait, so you're staking out the dock tonight?" Wendy asked.

"That's the idea," the sheriff said.

"I think it's worth a try," Terry said.

"How do you know he'll do it again tonight?" Wendy asked.

"I don't," Terry said. "But I've heard someone on the dock every three nights or so. Tonight would be the third night since last time, so ..."

"So you figure there's a decent chance," she said.

"I figure there's a decent chance," Terry said. The sheriff nodded in agreement.

"I want to come," she said.

"That's not a good idea, Wendy," the sheriff said. "He could be dangerous."

"You could be bored to death," Terry said.

"I still want to be there," she said.

Terry and the sheriff shared a look.

"OK, but be careful," the sheriff said.

"Yes!" Wendy said, pumping a fist. "I'll go grab my thermos. And my shotgun."

"Where's your gun, Terry?" the sheriff asked.

"What gun?" Terry asked.

The sheriff put his face in his hands.

•••

The three of them were in place, hiding out on *Easy Goer* and waiting in the cool, dark night. The lights of the marina reflected off the black surface of the water. They dared not talk, the only sounds being the water lapping against the hull and the creak of the dock floating on the surface.

It was well past 3 a.m. when they finally heard a new sound. It was the dock cart being pushed down the dock. Terry poked his head up and saw the silhouette of the cart and the person pushing it, past *Easy Goer* and down to the Sims's slip. The now familiar scent of decay hung heavily in the air. Wendy made a face in response.

The sheriff motioned for Terry to follow him, then stealthily climbed out of *Easy Goer's* cockpit. Terry followed, being careful with his weight. They didn't want the movement of the dock to tip off their quarry. Wendy, who was supposed to stay on the boat, followed next.

There, at the Sims's slip, was a tall, thin figure lifting something large and heavy in a garbage bag into the Chris-Craft cabin cruiser. He had it about chest-high when the sheriff, pointing his pistol at the figure, spoke quietly.

"Hold it right there," the sheriff said.

Dave Sims turned to see a cop holding him at gunpoint as he struggled to hold the garbage bag.

"Can I put this down?" Sims asked. "I think I'm gonna drop it."

"Slowly, and carefully," the sheriff said, his gun as steady as a mountain.

Sims set the cage down in the boat, then slowly straightened and raised his hands above his head.

"Terry," the sheriff said. "Grab my cuffs and secure Mr. Sims, please."

"Am I under arrest?" Sims asked.

"Not necessarily," the sheriff said as Terry took the cuffs off his belt and stepped over to Sims, taking his hands and lowering them behind his back, snapping the cuffs closed. Wendy was standing on the dock with her 870 Marine Magnum, light glinting off the silver rust-proof coating on the barrel. "This is just for our own protection, at the moment. We need to talk to you, Mr. Sims."

Once Sims was cuffed, the sheriff re-engaged the safety on his Beretta and put it back in its holster. He patted Sims down for a weapon, then walked over to the boat and opened one of the garbage bags. Inside, an old-fashioned round lobster cage containing the slightly bloated severed head of a pig. The stench wafted out considerably stronger, but the sheriff had smelled death before, and though he didn't enjoy it, it was amazing what the human mind can become accustomed to.

"OK," Sims grinned, turning to face the sheriff. "Let's talk."

"Wendy," the sheriff said. "You OK with us taking him back to the Reach for this."

"I get to bill the county for it?" she asked.

"No," the sheriff said.

"Oh, OK, fine. You did let me come along."

"Let's go," Tim said. "Terry, you lead us there. Sims, you're in front of me. Wendy, you follow me. And don't shoot me with that fucking cannon." He paused. "But shoot him if he tries to get away," he said, nodding toward Sims and winking.

"That won't be necessary," Sims said.

The foursome walked to the Beam Reach in the orangish sodium arc lighting of the marina's parking lot. Terry unlocked to door to the bar and led the group back to Wendy's office. Once inside, they put Sims in a chair, and Wendy plopped onto the couch across from him, her shotgun in her arms, not exactly pointed at Sims. But not exactly not pointed at Sims, either.

"Are these really necessary?" Sims asked, lifting his cuffed wrists behind his back. "They're really uncomfortable."

The sheriff closed the office door behind him and pulled Wendy's desk chair over so he could sit blocking the doorway.

"You can take them off," he said to Terry, tossing him a keyring.

Terry removed the cuffs and handed them and the sheriff's keys back to Tim.

"So, what do you want to talk about?" Sims asked, rubbing his wrists.

"Rincon Point?" the sheriff asked.

"You know what they did to Brandon?" Sims asked.

Both Terry and the sheriff nodded.

"Yeah, we know," the sheriff said. "I've had him looking into it, even though it's not my jurisdiction." Tim nodded in Terry's direction.

"Yeah, jurisdiction," Sims sneered. "Shit like that is why *I* had to do something. You cops weren't going to do a goddamned thing."

Tim gave Sims a disappointed look.

"I *am* doing something about it. But I have to operate within the bounds of the law. If I don't, we can't convict the bastards."

"Well, I don't have to worry about the bounds of law," Sims said.

"That's where you're wrong," the sheriff said. "But we'll get to that. Tell me what you've been doing."

"I'm wrong?" Sims said. "I'm not sure if you know this, but your man over there. Yeah, him," he said, looking at Terry. "Well, he's working for Vin Capriani on the side."

"As a matter of fact, I do know," the sheriff said. "I recommended him to Vin."

Sims couldn't have looked more stunned if he'd been told Santa Claus was real, and mixing drinks at the bar.

"So you guys are working for Vin?" Sims asked.

"He's working for Vin," the sheriff said. "I work for all the citizens of Ventura County. Vin is one of them."

"I am too," Sims said.

"So let me work for you," the sheriff said. "Tell me what you know."

"As a matter of fact, I do know something," Sims said.

"What have you been doing?" the sheriff asked.

"A little midnight lobster fishing off the coast of Rincon," Sims said.

"You know, lobster season doesn't start until October," the sheriff said.

"Guess I wasn't thinking about that when I set my traps."

"And those traps just happened to attract some sharks to the beach," the sheriff said.

"How was I to know?" Sims said. "But that's not the interesting part."

"I may differ with you there, but please continue," the sheriff said.

"Well, the other night, last time I was out, I saw someone dump a body."

That got everybody's attention.

"I'm listening," the sheriff said.

"It was a fishing boat named *Artemis*. I marked the spot on my chart."

33

Coming Together

The next morning saw Terry in Sheriff Baker's office. Neither man had gotten much sleep thanks to the activities of the night before at the marina, but both were running on a potent mix of adrenaline, caffeine and excitement. The hunt was on for real now, and they were energized by it.

"Glad you're here," Tim said to his friend, who had surprised him with his aptitude for deduction despite the high regard he thought he'd always held him in. "First things, first, come with me, please."

Terry followed the sheriff down to the basement of the government building, where the sheriff's department armory and shooting range were. The air down there was slightly humid, and thick with the acrid scent of spent gunpowder. They went through the range area and over to the armory, where a veteran deputy kept watch over the deadly inventory. He looked to be in his late 50s, white hair close cropped in a military buzz and a cheerful face despite years of having seen it all.

"Hey, Whiteside," the sheriff said. "We still got some of those surplus 92's?"

"Uh, yes, sir, sheriff," Deputy Whiteside said. "Guiberson's hasn't picked them up yet."

"How much are we getting for them?" the sheriff asked.

"Seventy-five bucks each," Whiteside replied.

The sheriff turned to Terry.

"You got $75?" the sheriff asked.

Terry pulled out his wallet and opened it.

"Uh, yeah," Terry said.

"Give it to Whiteside," the sheriff said.

Terry counted four $20 bills, slowly, as if it hurt to take each one from his wallet, then handed them over to Deputy Whiteside.

"Deputy," the sheriff said, "Log this as a surplus sale. Gimme one of those Berettas, and three mags to go with it."

Deputy Whiteside went back and rooted around for a while, coming back to the counter with a large, black automatic pistol and two spare magazines. The sheriff took the pistol and the mags, and handed them to Terry. The gun's finish was worn where it had sat in a deputy's holster for the last four years, but it appeared to be in otherwise good condition. Terry took the pistol, which already had its slide locked back, ejected the empty magazine, and worked the slide a couple of times. If felt right.

"I'm sure you've handled one of these before, back in the Army," the sheriff said to Terry.

"Actually, we hadn't made the transition yet when I was there," Terry said. "I carried an M1911, the old .45, you know. But some of the guys I knew were part of a group that was testing these. I never got to shoot one, but I've seen them."

"All right," the sheriff said. "Whiteside, let's get a couple boxes of nines, too, please."

Deputy Whiteside pulled two 50-round boxes of Federal Hydra-Shok 9mm ammunition from under the desk and put it on the counter for the sheriff. Then he retrieved five silhouette targets and put them on the counter too.

"Lane two is all yours, sir," Deputy Whiteside said.

"Let's go," the sheriff said to Terry, taking the ammo and the targets.

Tim attached a target to the hanger, then hit the switch to drag it back 10 yards. He pointed to the gun, magazines and ammo and looked at Terry.

"OK, load it up and let's see how you can handle it," he said.

Terry picked up the Beretta, hefted it. It was about the same size as the old .45 he was used to from his days in the Army guard shack, but thicker. But Terry had big hands, and the fat grip of the Beretta filled them pleasantly. He practiced aiming it down the range, still unloaded, just getting used to the grip and the layout of the sights, which stuck up a bit higher than the old Army M1911's.

"What about my five bucks?" Terry asked.

"Ammo," the sheriff said. Terry dropped the subject.

He put the pistol down, picked up a magazine, and loaded it with 15 rounds of the wicked looking hollow-points. He slammed the magazine home in the butt of the Italian automatic, then pointed it downrange and ripped the slide back, letting it crash forward on a fresh round. The gun was charged and ready to go. He aimed at the target, holding the pistol one-handed in a classic Army stance, and pulled the trigger. And nothing happened. The trigger went straight back without resistance. He looked at the side of the pistol, noticed the safety lever was down, flicked it off with his thumb, and tried again.

Terry put 13 of 15 round into a single hole the size of a half-dollar right in the 10-ring. The other two rounds made separate holes, each no more than half an inch from the larger one. He reloaded, then switched to his left hand and put another 15 rounds through the target's head, all in an area that could be covered by a pack of cigarettes.

"OK, I guess you know how to shoot," the sheriff said.

Terry looked back at the sheriff and grinned.

"I guess I never told you, but I qualified Expert with a pistol back in the Army.," Terry said. "That was fun. Man, I need to do this more often."

"Yes," the sheriff said. "If you need more ammo, go to Guiberson's Guns in Camarillo. They give a law-enforcement discount. You should probably get some kind of holster too. Now that you have a fucking gun, you do need to do this more often. Safe and stow that weapon, Cahill. And come with me."

Terry double checked to make sure that the gun was empty, then let the slide home on an empty mag, reengaged the safety, and stuffed the gun in the back of the waistband of his jeans. He picked up the boxes of ammunition and followed the sheriff back to his office.

"Place your right hand on this Bible," the sheriff said.

"Uh, you have a copy of the Constitution instead?" Terry asked.

"You prefer to swear on the Constitution?" the sheriff asked.

"It means more to me," Terry said. "I've already sworn an oath to preserve, protect and defend it, and I meant every last word of it. I consider it a sacred document."

"Fine," the sheriff said. He went to the bookshelf behind his desk and pulled out a pocket copy of the U.S. Constitution. "Place your right hand on the Constitution, please, and repeat after me."

Terry placed his hand on the Constitution.

"I, 'your name,'" the sheriff said.

"I, Terrance Marshall Cahill," Terry said.

"Having been appointed reserve deputy sheriff of Ventura County."

"Having been appointed reserve deputy sheriff of Ventura County," Terry said, with a quizzical look on his face.

"Do solemnly swear that I will truly and faithfully enter and record all orders, decrees, judgments and proceedings of such office, and will faithfully and impartially discharge all other duties of my office according to the best of my abilities and understanding. So help me God."

Terry repeated the oath, still surprised by this development.

"I hereby declare you reserve deputy sheriff of Ventura County, with all the powers, privileges and duties therein. Congratulations, Terry. You have just been legally deputized." He pulled a badge from his desk drawer and handed it to Terry.

"Holy shit," Terry said.

"Yeah, it's a big responsibility," the sheriff said. "But I think you can handle it. And by the way, I expect you to keep that weapon on you at all times until this thing is over, understood? I have a hunch that things are going to get dangerous. Try not to get busted with it, but if you do, flash the tin."

"Just one question? What does 'reserve' mean?"

"It means you don't get paid. Now, let's call Decker."

• • •

"Detective Decker," Terry heard over the sheriff's speakerphone.

"Decker, it's Sheriff Baker, of Ventura County," Tim said.

"Sheriff," Decker said. "To what do I owe the call?"

"Detective, I think it's time we have a little powwow. You got a couple hours to burn today?"

"You know better, sheriff," Decker said. "I'm working multiple homicides. I don't have a spare couple of seconds."

"Well, we think we can help you down here. Why don't you carve out some time and come on over. It should be worth your while."

"Is that an order?"

"You know I can't order you to do shit. Consider it an official request, one that may help you clear up those murders."

"What do you have, sheriff?" Decker asked.

"You heard of a fishing boat named *Artemis*?"

"I'm listening."

"Come on down, detective. We have some things to discuss."

"I can be there in an hour," Decker said.

"We'll see you then," the sheriff said, then hung up. "Load that weapon, Cahill," he said to Terry. "It doesn't do any good without bullets."

• • •

Detective Decker arrived just less than an hour after the sheriff's call. He walked into the office, shook hands with Sheriff Baker, then saw Terry sitting in the office.

"What is he doing here?" Decker asked.

"He's with us," the sheriff said.

"Not good enough," Decker said.

"I've officially deputized him," the sheriff said. "From here on, you can consider him a fellow cop."

"But he's not a cop," Decker protested.

"I say he is," the sheriff said. Terry flashed his badge. "So does that badge."

"Well, I guess that's good enough for me," Decker said in defeat.

"No guessing," the sheriff said. "He is."

Decker raised his hands.

"OK, he's a cop."

"Good," the sheriff said. Terry just observed the exchange, not wanting to make things more difficult.

"So," Decker said, "What have you got for me?"

"You know about a fishing vessel named *Artemis*." the sheriff began.

Decker visibly sharpened at that, and both Terry and the sheriff noticed.

• • •

"I knew something was up with Brad Keener," Decker said.

Terry and the sheriff waited patiently for Decker to continue.

"Brad Keener, half-owner of Shockley's Tavern," Decker said. "Went missing four days ago. His boat, *Artemis*, was found by a Coast Guard patrol, apparently abandoned. No sign of Keener. But ..."

"But what?" Terry asked.

"But the keys were gone when the Coast Guard boarded the boat. No sign of Keener. No signs of foul play on the boat. There were traces of blood, but not human. Fishing boat. Fish blood. No drugs, no nothing, at least on the boat."

"Not on the boat," Terry said. "Sounds like you found something, somewhere."

"I did," Decker said. "Keener's car was parked at the marina."

"Well, it would be if he went out on his boat and something happened," the sheriff said, knowing he was leading Decker along his own path of discovery.

"Keener drove a Ramcharger, you know?" Decker said. "It's a four-by-four, an SUV. I took a look inside. Not much to find. But in the back, the cargo area ..."

Terry and the sheriff waited.

"In the cargo area, there's carpet," Decker said. "In the carpet, there were some impressions. On the right side, a couple of large round impressions, and some writing. It was from weights, like you'd see in a gym. Ten kilos each. And on the other side, a cross-hatch pattern."

He looked at the sheriff, and then Terry.

"A cross-hatch pattern like a large fish net," Decker continued.

He saw the recognition on both men's faces.

"As if a body were dumped at sea," Decker said.

"Yeah, we got that," the sheriff said. It was his turn to stun Decker. "We have a witness to the possible body dump, roughly three miles off the coast of Rincon at approximately 4 a.m., four nights ago. The vessel our witness saw was a pleasure fishing boat named *Artemis*."

"*Artemis*. Brad Keener's boat," Decker said.

"And Keener's been missing since when?" Terry asked.

"Since the night your witness saw something," Decker said.

"Isn't that a coincidence?" Terry asked.

"No," Decker said. "It's not."

"I think we should work together, don't you, Detective Decker?" the sheriff asked.

"Yeah," Decker said. "I think it's time we do. Let me tell you what I know about the killing of Jonathan Abernathy."

When Detective Decker was done recounting the story of Abernathy's murder in his hospital bed, Terry spoke up.

"Latex gloves," Terry said.

"Yeah, that was the big clue," Decker said. "Without that, I don't know that anything else would have prompted suspicion in Abernathy's death."

"I was just thinking," Terry continued. "I know hospitals don't use latex because of the allergen issue. But you know who do still use latex gloves?" It wasn't really a question.

"Cops," Sheriff Baker said.

Decker nodded in agreement.

"So we're all thinking the same thing here." Terry said.

...

Terry, Sheriff Baker, and Detective Decker all drove over to the Docksider Motel, where David Sims was being held in protective custody as a material witness. The sheriff had arranged a deal for Sims with Deputy District Attorney Shannon Kallin in which he exchanged his potential testimony in court for immunity from prosecution himself. Though neither told Sims this, both were relieved that they could make the deal, as there was some question of exactly what to charge Sims with beyond fishing out of season and without a license, and how strong a case they had against him if they did bring charges. Still, DDA Kallin was looking into it, just in case Sims didn't come through.

The interview was brief. Sims recounted his story for Detective Decker, and showed him the nautical chart where Sims had marked the position of *Artemis* on the night of Brad Keener's disappearance. He then identified a photo of Jonathan Abernathy as the man who assaulted Brandon Capriani at Rincon Point. Decker had a few questions, but no new ground was covered.

"I don't like giving that kid immunity," Decker said as he was walking out to the motel parking lot with Terry and the sheriff. "He's a killer. Two people have died because of what he did."

"I'm not in love with it either," Tim said. "But the unfortunate reality is that it would be a tricky prosecution at best, and he might be the key to catching another killer who is far more dangerous."

"Yeah," Decker grunted. "I don't like it, but the alternative may be worse." Decker was getting into his unmarked Caprice when he pointed over at Sheriff Baker's patrol car. "How do you like the Shamu?" he asked.

Baker looked over at his car.

"It's not pretty, that's for sure," the sheriff said. "But that Corvette motor under the hood more than makes up for it."

"Yeah, I hear they're pretty quick," Decker said. "We're supposed to be getting Crown Vics next year."

"The Fords are usually a little better built," the sheriff said. "But the Chevys are almost always faster. Me, I'll take the extra power."

"My Buick'll smoke 'em both," Terry said. "High-compression four fifty-five, Stage I."

"Yeah, that piece of shit probably passes everything but a gas station," Decker said.

"It gets even faster as parts of it rust away or fall off," the sheriff said.

"Don't listen to them, hon," Terry said to his Electra. "They're just jealous."

34

Wet Work

Detective Rick Decker drove back up to Santa Barbara and straight to the Coast Guard station at the marina. He wanted to enlist their help in finding and hopefully removing the lobster cages Dave Sims had deposited off the coast of Rincon Point. He also wanted to see if there were any chance of recovering Brad Keener's body.

Master Chief Donnelly shot a few holes in those hopes.

"We might be able to retrieve the cages," Donnelly said. "You'd be surprised at how much junk is down there, though. It'll be tough to find them in all the clutter, but the water should be shallow enough to at least give it a try."

"And Keener?" Decker asked.

"Forget it. Three miles offshore? That's past the shelf, and the water is too deep there. And that's if currents haven't moved the body somewhere else, which, they probably have. Or if predators haven't found the body and eaten it, which I also wouldn't bet against, especially with the recent shark activity in the area. If Keener got dropped out there, he's gone.

"By the way," Donnelly continued. "The marina reported an ocean-going kayak missing yesterday."

"Really," Decker said. "How long has it been missing?"

"Near as they can figure it, about four days or so."

"Why didn't they report it sooner?"

"Well, the kayaks are there on a rack, free to use for anyone with a slip at the marina. Sometimes people take 'em out for a weekend trip. They probably didn't know it was missing for a while."

"But nobody brought it back?"

"No. The harbormaster did a little look around, didn't see it on anyone's boat. Could have been lost or something, and just not reported."

"Yeah," Decker said. "Could have been."

• • •

It was a man walking his dog illegally on Silver Strand Beach in Oxnard who found the arm. It was bleached and bloated, half-buried in the sand, and appeared to have been gnawed off at the shoulder joint by something large. He had to restrain his German Sheppard to keep it from picking up the gruesome artifact. As he was struggling with the dog, he noticed a glint of light reflecting from a gold ring on the third finger.

The dog-walker phoned in an anonymous tip to the Ventura County Sheriff's Department and told them where to find it. Deputy Lee Ramirez was dispatched to the beach. He radioed the sheriff's office and requested to speak with Sheriff Baker when he saw that the arm was indeed real.

"You're going to want to see this," Deputy Ramirez said.

"Crime scene unit is on its way. I'll come down and have a look, too. And thank you, deputy. You did good to call me on this."

Terry met Sheriff Baker at the morgue.

"It's Keener," the sheriff said. "We've found him, well, part of him."

"Enough for proof of death?" Terry asked.

"Probably, yeah."

"How do we know it's Keener? Prints?"

The sheriff pulled a small plastic evidence bag from his pocket. Inside was a USC class ring, class of '82.

"Keener's class ring," the sheriff said. "There's an inscription on the inside, the part normally hidden when it's worn."

Terry looked at the ring. He could read the inscription through the bag.

"Congrats, Brad! Love, mom and dad."

He looked up at the sheriff.

"OK, I'm convinced. You tell Decker about this yet?"

"Yeah. The ring is staying here for now as evidence, since it washed up on the coast of my county. We took prints from the hand, but we'll need Santa Barbara to dust his house to get a comparison. Even then, the skin might be too waterlogged to get usable prints at this point. But we've already had the ring photographed, and I have a deputy couriering copies up to Santa Barbara. He's going to show them to family, friends of Keener for a positive ID. I don't think there's any doubt what they'll find."

"Me either. OK, so we have a body, we have a murder victim, and we have a witness. All we need now is the killer."

"That's usually the difficult part," the sheriff said.

• • •

Detective Decker had been disappointed by what he'd learned at the Coast Guard station, but not terribly surprised. On the bright side, the station commander agreed to send a boat out to try and retrieve the lobster cages that were attracting unwelcome visitors to Rincon. They were using sonar and a powerful magnet on the end of a long cable, and pulling up all kinds of crap with it. Some of it was even what they were there to search for.

Sheriff Baker's call lifted his spirits considerably. Now he had evidence that Keener was dead, and dumped offshore just as the witness Sims had claimed. He could feel the case taking on a momentum of its own.

There was, however, still something troubling him. He was starting to look at his fellow cops as suspects. And he couldn't help hearing the voice from his gut saying Deputy Kirkham stood out in that group. He apparently had connections, either direct or adjacent, to all of the victims, including Danielle Winfield. Decker had looked at the police report on the Winfield incident and noticed the names of the witnesses. They were Dewey Michaels, Shane Larson, William Newhouse, and Jonathan Abernathy.

Keener and Newhouse had been bartenders at Shockley's Tavern at the time of Winfield's death. Neither man mentioned that Winfield had been drinking at Shockley's the night before she died. Six months later, Margate Bank made a substantial business loan to William Newhouse, and Newhouse and Keener went in together to buy Shockley's Tavern. Decker smelled a payoff.

Decker thought he knew pretty well what had happened. Abernathy was drugging women and sexually assaulting them at Shockley's Tavern, probably with the assistance of Newhouse and maybe Keener. Winfield had traded her spiked drink with Anna Henley because it tasted off, not knowing the drink had been tampered with. Then Winfield embarrassed Abernathy in front of the crowd at Shockley's, and Abernathy was ejected from the bar.

Henley passed out hard from the dosed drink and didn't wake up in time to join Winfield at the beach. Winfield went to Rincon Point to surf alone, where she encountered Abernathy, Newhouse, Larson and Michaels. The other three were planning their usual intimidation tactics, but Abernathy, enraged from the night before, went too far and killed the young woman, possibly by hitting her on the head with a surfboard and drowning her.

Deputy Kerry Kirkham, also a surfer, responded to the call and found his friends on the beach with a dead body. The five men then engaged in a criminal conspiracy to cover up the crime as an accident. William

Newhouse asked for, and received a bribe in the form of a loan from Margate Bank, likely expedited by Dewey Michaels, in exchange for his silence. He then used that money for his half of Shockley's Tavern.

And then? Everything was more or less quiet for the next seven years. Abernathy and the other Santa Barbara Boys continued their intimidation and assaults on surfers unwise or unaware enough to visit Rincon, but nothing makes very big waves. Then Abernathy went too far again, putting the son of a Mafia kingpin in the hospital. Brandon Capriani's friend, David Sims, then responded by baiting sharks near the beach. Abernathy was attacked by a shark, lost his leg, and ended up in the hospital himself.

The killer, Kirkham as Decker was thinking of it, saw this as an opportunity to rid the group of Abernathy. His uncontrollable violence had been the start of all of this trouble, and his actions with drugging and assaulting women were also problematic. Abernathy was going to get busted for something sooner or later, and when he did it was reasonable to expect that others would be taken down with him. Kirkham may have even known whom Brandon Capriani was. If so, he then had not only the law, but the mob to worry about.

So Kirkham smothered Abernathy in the hospital with a pillow. And he almost got away with it, except he wore the wrong gloves without knowing it. Doctor Kreutz picked up on the rash, suspected foul play, and performed an autopsy confirming Abernathy was murdered. Instead of silencing things once and for all, Abernathy's murder brought more questions.

Meanwhile the smartass ex-reporter from Ventura started sniffing around the beach at Rincon. He and his buddies beat the shit out of a few Santa Barbara Boys on their own turf, and one of them, Scott Keener, started talking a little too much to Cahill. That night, Kirkham visits the younger Keener brother, kills him, and tries to stage the death as a suicide.

But Kirkham fucked up again, and the suicide story wasn't bought. Brad Keener suspected someone in the Santa Barbara Boys of killing his brother. So he contacted the reporter Cahill and told him about the Winfield murder. Why call the reporter and not the cops? A couple of reasons came to Decker, but the most likely to him was that Keener knew it would get back to Kirkham. Then Keener got disappeared.

Decker didn't know how Keener was murdered, but he let that go for the moment. Kirkham somehow lured Keener to his death, probably killed him where they met and put the body in the back of the victim's car. He drove the body to the marina, where he transferred it to *Artemis*, wrapped it in a fishing net, and weighted it down with barbell weights. He dumped the body offshore, where David Sims witnessed the drop. Then he took the boat closer in to the shore and abandoned it.

How did he get off the boat? Probably a dinghy or something like that. Maybe the missing kayak? However he did it, Kirkham returned to shore, went back to his own car, and drove away. If the meeting point had been at Shockley's, that was only a mile from the beach in Carpinteria. He could have walked back there easily. Decker made a note to see if Shockley's had a security camera on the parking lot. He also thought it would be good to send a forensics team to check the lot for blood. Not that he expected to find it so much, but seeing them might put a scare into Newhouse, and that would be good for Decker's purposes.

…

Terry called Vin from the Beam Reach after his meeting with the sheriff. He figured it was about time to update the man who was paying him.

"What's up, kid?" Vin said. "You got something for me?"

"Yes," Terry said. "Can we meet somewhere?"

"Meet me at the hospital. I'm going over to visit Brandon. Was just heading out when you called."

"I can be there in 10 minutes."

"See you then."

He walked into the hospital room at the appointed time to find Vin uncharacteristically cheerful. The big man walked over to Terry and gave him a bear hug.

"My boy's recovering," Vin said. "The doctors took him out of the coma yesterday. He's groggy as hell, sleeps a lot of the time, but I got to talk to him yesterday. He remembers me."

"That's great news, Vin," Terry said. "I'm glad to hear it." He looked over at the young man, sleeping in his nest of IVs and and wires. "I hope what I have to say will also be received as good news."

"Ha, Cahill. Always talking like a writer. What did you want to tell me?"

"We know who attacked Brandon and his friend at the beach. We've made a positive ID."

"And the law is going after the fuck, right?"

"Actually, the guy who did it is dead."

Terry let that news settle a bit before continuing.

"You've heard about the shark attacks lately up at Rincon?" Terry asked.

Vin nodded.

"Your son's friend, Dave Sims, was taking his parents' boat out late at night and dropping lobster cages full of rotting meat a couple hundred yards off the shore. He was baiting sharks. The bait worked.

"The man who hurt your son was named Jonathan Abernathy. A shark bit his leg off. He died in the hospital. But Abernathy and his friends were involved in a bit more than that. I can't tell you much about that yet, but it's an ongoing criminal investigation. The authorities are going after the rest of the group."

"How hard are they going after these guys?" Vin asked.

"There are going to be multiple murder charges," Terry said. "They're going all the way."

Vin let out a low whistle.

"So, you think it's safe to say that they're fucked?" Vin said.

"Fucked sideways."

"What about you? I see you're carrying a piece now."

"I didn't think you'd notice."

"Piece that big is hard to conceal."

"That's what all the girls say."

Vin laughed.

"Forty-five?" Vin asked.

"Beretta."

"Nice choice. You should get a holster, though. Things heating up, you need any protection?"

"It's just a precaution," Terry said. "Sheriff thought it'd be a good idea for the time being. But I appreciate the offer. There is one thing, though."

"Speak."

"Dave Sims, the kid who did the shark thing. He has a deal with the DDA as a witness against these guys. He should have immunity. But sometimes, deals fall through. I'm sure you know a good lawyer or two. Maybe it wouldn't be a bad idea to keep that in mind, just in case."

"I can do that."

35

Intimidation

Decker was at his desk in the Santa Barbara Sheriff's Department office. He hadn't been spending much time there lately, but his presence this time was deliberate. When he heard Deputy Kirkham hanging around, he had his cue. He stood up, carrying a manilla envelope containing the pictures of Brad Keener's ring and severed arm. He went over to the coffee maker Kirkham was standing near.

"Afternoon, Rick," Kirkham said.

"Afternoon, Kerry, How's your day going?"

"Another day in paradise. Can't complain. How's yours?"

"Not gonna lie, it's gonna be a rough one, I'm afraid. I gotta go talk to the family and friends of another murder victim, show them some nasty photographs. I hate this shit, you know?"

"Yeah, that's ... well, nobody likes that part of the job."

Decker pulled the images out of the envelope and showed Deputy Kirkham. The first one was of the arm.

"Look at that," Decker said. "That's all that's left of Brad Keener." He was studying Kirkham's face for a reaction. Kirkham grimaced appropriately.

"Jesus, that is nasty," Kirkham said.

Decker pulled out one of the pictures of the class ring.

"This is what identified him at first. Skin may be too far gone to get any usable prints, but we'll see. Anyway, we have the ring. I have to talk to some people, make sure, but there was an inscription inside, and Keener was at 'SC, class of '82. We're pretty sure at this point it's him. Just making the confirmation."

"Any leads?"

"I think it's the same person who did his brother, and Abernathy too. You know what that means?"

Kirkham just looked at the detective.

"Three bodies, special circumstances," Decker said. "It means this guy is gonna get the gas for this, when we catch him."

"That's ..."

"I ever tell you I witnessed an execution once?" Decker asked. "Up at Quentin."

"Uh, no, you never told me that."

"Back in '67. I had just made detective, back when I was with LAPD. This prick, Michael Allan Dunphy, had shot my partner when I was a patrol officer. Killed him right there. I shot him in the gut, but he survived it. Docs patched him up just so he could get executed. Two-bit hood, fleeing a robbery. Had a sheet a mile long. I thought I'd feel some sense of justice seeing him get it.

"It was fucking awful. It was the worst thing I've ever seen, and I've worked my share of homicides, seen more than my share of dead bodies. But watching a man die like that? I'll never do that again. You know, they don't show you the part where they lead him to the chamber, strap him in and all that. They just open a curtain, and there he is. They don't hood 'em in the gas chamber 'cause some of the gas might get trapped under it. You can see his face, his eyes.

"He was scared shitless. They keep it warm in the chamber, and humid. The gas works best that way. There were beads of sweat all over him. Eyes as big as saucers. He can't move. Can't do shit but wait to die. That's the other thing; they don't just strap him in, shut the door, and let the gas go. He sat there strapped in to that airtight chamber where he would die, must've been ten minutes, maybe longer, just sitting there being stared at by the people who came to see him gasp for his last breath, sweating bullets. You could see the sweat running into his eyes, but he couldn't wipe it away because his hands were strapped down to the chair. And dangling underneath that chair, a little cheesecloth bag full of cyanide pellets, just waiting to be dipped into a bath of acid.

"Finally, the time comes. No call from the governor. They pulled the lever. The gas pellets dropped into the acid. I could've sworn I could hear the hiss, but maybe it was my imagination. The executioners, when they're strapping 'em in, they tell them to take a deep breath when the gas comes, say it'll go easier that way. You could see Dunphy struggle with the decision. They say some of them hold their breath for as long as they can. Dunphy decided to take the breath.

"I saw him breathe in that first lungful of poison, and I could tell right away he regretted it. His eyes bulged, he started to twitch. A couple more breaths and he's foaming at the mouth. He starts to retch, throws up his last meal all over himself, but he can't stop. He's foaming and puking, his eyes look like they're going to pop out of his head. I could see the veins standing out on his forehead. He starts throwing his head, back and forth, violently. Still puking up little bits here and there. Can't control it.

"But his eyes. His eyes were still open. He was still conscious. We all knew it. Even when his face turned purple, he was still awake. It took him 21 minutes to die in there. He was there for most of it. I have no doubt that it was incredibly painful. Twenty-one minutes of basically torture. Those were his last moments alive.

"I'll tell you this: If I ever were gonna go down and knew that was what was waiting for me, I'd never let them take me. I'd eat my fucking gun first. The gas chamber is barbaric. I had nightmares about it for years.

"Anyway, I'll see you around," Decker said, putting the pictures back in the envelope as he walked away.

· · ·

Decker's next stop was Shockley's Tavern. The forensics team was already there, the entire parking lot roped off with police tape. Decker parked at the curb and brought the envelope with the pictures inside. Billy Newhouse was there, behind the bar. Decker approached.

"Mr. Newhouse," Decker said. "I've got some images here I'd like you to take a look at. We need your help in identifying your former partner, Brad Keener."

"Uh ..." Newhouse said.

Decker hit him first with the severed arm image.

"How the fuck am I supposed to identify that?" Newhouse asked. He looked pretty green around the gills.

"Well, for one, did Keener have any tattoos or identifying marks on his right arm?"

"No."

"OK, then. Do you recognize this ring?" Decker showed him the next couple of images.

"Yeah," Newhouse said. "Yeah, Brad had a ring like that."

"Just like it?"

"Yeah, just like it. School colors, cardinal and gold."

"You ever see the inscription inside it?"

"No, he didn't really take it off in my presence."

"That's OK, we'll ask his parents."

"Do you know what happened?" Newhouse asked. "I mean, how he ended up ..."

"Dead?" Decker said. "Yeah, we have a pretty good idea. He was murdered. Then he was dumped somewhere in the ocean."

What color was left in Newhouse's face drained. He was almost as white as Keener's severed arm.

"Don't leave town anytime soon, Mr. Newhouse," Decker said. "We may need to ask you some more questions."

He left the bar and went back out to his car.

36

Out Of The Frying Pan

Terry woke up to *Easy Goer* gently rocking in the waves created by the wake of a boat leaving the harbor. He looked up to see Charlie the dock cat curled up at his feet. The cat woke up too and lifted his head.

"Good morning, Charlie," Terry said.

"Mrow," replied the cat. He looked happy.

Terry sat up in the berth and gave the cat some head scratches, which the cat gracefully accepted. After a few minutes of that, the cat stood up, stretched, and hopped down, pawing at the door to get out.

"Yeah," Terry said. "I suppose it is breakfast time."

He let the cat out and went back to the galley to nuke up some tea. He thought about getting a newspaper, but decided he could do that while he was out.

After relaxing in the cockpit with his tea, watching boats go out to sea, he got ready for his day. While he enjoyed mornings on the boat, the walk to the marina bathroom every morning was getting tiresome. He missed having a place where he could walk to the shower without having to get dressed first.

Cleaned up, shaved, and ready to go, he put on a pair of jeans and a vintage Keith Black Racing Engines t-shirt, then a lightweight sport coat to cover the handgun he wasn't used to carrying. Stuffing the big automatic in the waistband of his pants was not a great way to lug the thing around. He decided he'd go down to Camarillo to see about getting some kind of holster.

• • •

The drive down the 101 to the Old Town Camarillo district was uneventful. He parked his Buick at the curb on Ventura Boulevard in front of Guiberson's, a small gun store in a building hosting four other businesses. Inside, Terry was greeted by a large bearded man. Terry introduced himself and showed the man his badge.

"Anthony Guiberson," the man said, holding out his hand. Terry shook it.

"You the owner?" Terry asked.

"No, that'd be my father. But I can help you with whatever you need."

"Well, I need some kind of holster for a Beretta."

"92?"

"Yeah."

"What kinda rig are you looking for?"

"Something comfortable, hopefully unobtrusive. It'd be good if it weren't obvious I'm carrying."

"With a Beretta 92?" Guiberson laughed. "You ever think about carrying a smaller gun?"

"I'm pretty new to the whole carrying a gun all the time thing, actually. This is what I've got. I was hoping to find a way to make it work."

"Well, you've got a few options. Probably the easiest and most comfortable would be a clip-on worn on your hip. That's also the least concealable, though. You could do a shoulder rig, some guys find the straps uncomfortable, others don't mind it. But you'd always have to wear a jacket over it if you don't want people to see it. They're also the most expensive option."

"I'm not a real big fan of the most expensive option, generally speaking."

"Then there's one that clips on the inside of your pants. Probably the least comfortable for a big gun like that, but the easiest to conceal. It'd still be better than carrying it in your waistband, though."

Terry tried on a few different holsters. When they got to the shoulder setup, he said: "No thanks. I don't want to spend the money. Or look like a Don Johnson wannabe."

He eventually decided on a Galco leather holster that attached to his belt via loops. It was a good compromise between the comfort of the clip-on style, and the less conspicuous profile of the inside-the-waistband one. He also picked up a couple of extra boxes of Federal Hydra-Shok 9mm ammunition. The tab added up to more than he'd paid for the gun.

Terry left the gun store wearing his Beretta in the new holster. He stowed the ammo in the car's cavernous trunk, then got into his Buick and headed back up the 101 for Ventura. As he was pulling away from the curb, he noticed a black LS400 doing the same a few spots behind him.

Man, those things are everywhere, he thought.

He exited Seaward Avenue and went toward the marina. He had an afternoon shift at the Beam Reach. He decided he could lock the gun in Wendy's desk while he worked.

• • •

Shockley's Tavern hadn't opened for the day yet. Billy Newhouse and Brad Keener had been the only managers at the bar, and with Keener dead Newhouse had trimmed back the less profitable daytime hours on weekdays, opting to run the bar himself on nights and weekends.

Newhouse was there with Jeremey Dodd, Don Harris and Pete Edwards. They were drinking beers in the closed bar and shooting the shit. The conversation had been about Keener.

"You think those guys from the beach had something to do with it?" Harris asked.

"Somebody did," Dodd said. "Look, those guys came up here, beat us up. Next thing you know, somebody kills Brad and dumps him in the ocean. I don't know anyone around here with the balls to do that."

"I don't know about that," Newhouse said.

"You know anyone else who'd want to off Brad?" Dodd asked.

"No."

"I heard a rumor that reporter guy is connected," Harris said.

"Connected like how?" Edwards asked.

"Like, mobbed up," Harris said.

"Where the fuck would you hear something like that?" Newhouse asked.

Harris shrugged. "I called the paper down in Ventura where he supposedly works. Guy who answered said, 'Never heard of him. Why don't you try asking the Capriani family?' I didn't know what he meant at first. Then I remembered Capriani was the name of that mobster's kid we knocked out."

"So you think those guys on the beach ..." Dodd didn't finish his thought.

"I dunno, maybe," Harris said.

"Jesus!" Edwards said. "I wouldn't believe that, except ..."

"Except they've already fed one of us to the fuckin' sharks." Dodd said.

"What about the rest of us?" Edwards asked. "Are they gonna take us all out?"

"Not if we do something about it first," Dodd said.

"Do something?" Edwards asked. "Like what?"

"I did some digging around in public records," Harris said. "Found an address for a TAMBO Industries in Ventura, over by the pier. And get this: The company was founded by a Domonic Tambolini. Fuckin' greaseball name if you ask me. I think it's some kind of front."

"Yeah," Dodd said. "Don tracked them down. Now if we go down there, ski masks, guns, catch them when they're not expecting us ..."

"I'm not shooting anybody," Newhouse said.

"I'm not talking about shooting them," Dodd said. "Just let 'em know we mean business. See what kind of information we can get out of them, scare the shit out of them."

"I don't think these guys are gonna be that easy to scare if they're mob guys," Edwards said.

"They bleed like anyone else," Dodd said.

"I think you've had too many beers," Newhouse said. "That is the mother of all bad ideas. Count me the fuck out." He went back to the cooler to grab a case of Budweiser and start stocking the beer wells.

Dodd waited for Newhouse to be out of earshot, then said: "Look, the thing about mob guys is, they're not that tough ..."

• • •

Kerry Kirkham was spooked by his conversation with Decker. Everything he'd done to protect himself seemed to be backfiring, and he could feel the weight of his actions and their possible consequences.

He had been pretty sure he hadn't left behind any physical evidence linking him to any of the killings. He'd worn gloves, never used a gun or a weapon that could be traced back to him, there was no blood. Any case against him would have to be entirely circumstantial. But still.

Why would he tell me that shit about the gas chamber unless ...

Unless he fucked up.

Still, he had one more move left. He knew one thing about witnesses, and that was their testimony didn't mean much if they couldn't appear in court. He decided to take one last chance and made a call to a friend at the DMV.

• • •

Terry swung by *Easy Goer* after his shift at the bar to change clothes. He was going to meet Lance and the guys for some training that night. He knew he wasn't in the same physical condition he'd been in back in the army, and saw a night of exertion ahead of him, probably to be followed by a morning of sore muscles. Still, he found himself welcoming the opportunity. Too much bar food and too many nights of drinking needed some kind of balancing out.

He put on some khaki shorts and a fresh shirt to get rid of the booze and smoke smell from the bar, grabbed a towel, and headed up to the parking lot. He wasn't used to the gun he was wearing on his hip, but he figured that was just a temporary thing. He thought about walking there, but decided he wouldn't feel like walking back at the end of the night, so he hopped in the Buick and cruised across the 101 to Front Street and parked in front of the VPBJJ dojo. Lance greeted him at the door.

"My man!" Lance said, grinning.

"You guys gonna kick my ass tonight?" Terry asked.

"Nah, that comes later. Tonight we're going to start off slow. Come on back."

Terry followed him back into the dojo where Marcel and Brian were hanging out and exchanged greetings.

"OK, so, most basic of basics," Lance said. "We are going to start off tonight with some breathing exercises."

"I'm not gonna end up waxing your cars, am I?"

The guys all laughed.

"Seriously, though, you can't breathe, you can't fight. You need to be getting a good supply of oxygen to your muscles and your brain. It's the first step to physical conditioning, and we take it seriously here."

"So, what kind of training do you do here?" Terry asked.

"Commercially, we specialize in Brazilian Ju Jitsu. That's what we teach our students, and what we train the local cops on. It's largely based on submission holds, kinda like wrestling. Good for situations where you don't want to take too much chance of getting sued for excessive force. Privately, we work on all kinds of ass-kicking. Kenpo, boxing, Krav Maga, Muay Thai, even weapons training."

"I think what I learned in the Army falls under that 'other kinds of ass-kicking' category. You don't worry too much about getting sued by enemy combatants."

"We'll keep that in mind when it's time to spar," Lance said.

"Which won't be tonight."

"No, we want to get you in shape first. We'll work on breathing, then we'll have you jump rope for a while, maybe do some speed bag exercises."

"Well, OK, then. Got some place I can put this?" Terry pointed to his gun.

"You can put it in the office with mine," Lance said.

The office was behind a door off the long hallway. There was an old-fashioned wooden desk in there with an office chair that had seen better days about 40 or 50 years ago. Lance opened a desk drawer and Terry put his gun there next to a gun-shaped object wrapped in an oily rag. He didn't want his pager getting in the way, so he put that in the desk drawer too.

• • •

Deputy Kirkham wasn't the only one talking to the DMV. Detective Decker had put a flag on some names, requesting he be contacted directly if anyone tried to access their records. His bet paid off when the phone rang.

"We got some activity on one of the names you flagged," the DMV clerk told him.

"Which one?" Decker asked.

"Cahill, Terrance Marshall, of Ventura."

"Who put in the request?"

"That would be a Deputy Kirkham, out of Santa Barbara."

"OK, thanks. How much did he get?"

"Driver's license info, photo, address, the usual."

"When did the request come in?"

"Looks like it happened a few hours ago, this afternoon."

"Shit. I gotta make a phone call. Thanks."

Decker was miffed that he wasn't alerted sooner. He hoped it wasn't too late. He dialed Sheriff Baker's home phone number.

"Sheriff Baker, this is Rick Decker."

The sheriff sounded concerned. He knew if Decker was calling him at home, it wouldn't be to share good news.

"What's going on, detective?" Baker asked.

"I caught one of our deputies sniffing around DMV records for Cahill. He's got a photo and an address."

"Shit. That's not comforting."

"Sheriff, I'm looking at this guy as a suspect in the murders up here. I don't have anything concrete. More of a gut feeling and a few too many coincidences. But I don't like this."

"You contact Cahill about it?"

"No, I called you first."

"OK. I'll get in touch with him."

• • •

Terry was already worn out an hour after arriving at the dojo. After 20 minutes of relearning how to breathe, he'd jumped rope until his legs felt like jelly, then they made him do pull ups until his arms felt about the same. He was ready for a break.

"OK, I think that's enough of that," Lance said, bringing him a towel.

"Oh, thank fuck," Terry said. "I don't think I could take any more."

"Give us a month and we'll have you doing this shit for fun. You hungry?"

"Starving."

"We're thinking about some subs and a couple beers from Delissi's next door."

"I'll buy," Terry said.

"My man," Lance said.

Terry got the sandwich orders from the other guys and walked over to Delissi's to pick up the food.

・・・

While Terry was waiting on sandwiches, another car pulled up in front of the dojo with its lights turned off. Two men wearing black ski masks and carrying shotguns got out and hurried to the door. Terry hadn't locked it on his way out. The two men stepped inside and walked down the long hallway, stopping at the entrance of the dojo. They racked their shotguns, and Lance, Brian, and Marcel, who'd expected nothing more lethal than some hoagies, were taken entirely by surprise.

"I don't know who the fuck you dickbrains are, but you picked the wrong place to rob tonight," Lance said.

"We're not here to rob you, asshole."

・・・

Terry came out of Delissi's with a box of sandwiches and beer in his arms. He noticed the dojo's front door wasn't closed all the way and thought, *Was that me? I thought I closed that.*

He pushed the door open and saw two men in black clothes who appeared to be holding guns pointed into the dojo.

Shit! he thought. Then he reached down to his hip, where his gun wasn't.

Shit! he thought again.

Quickly, he came up with a plan. It wasn't a great plan, but he wasn't going to just walk away. He put down the box as quietly as he could, and pulled one of the beer bottles out. He hoped the gunmen's attention was focused in front of them as he crept toward the office door in the hallway. If he could get there, he could get to his gun. He might have a chance.

He knew the door opening would attract attention his way, but that was part of his plan. He hoped. When he got to the office door, he put his left hand on the door knob. He raised his right hand with the bottle of Pabst in it, and hurled it at the gunman on his left.

Jeremey Dodd literally didn't know what hit him. The ice-cold missile nailed him right in the back of the head, then clattered to the floor fizzing beer angrily from its cap. Dodd fell to his knees stunned, dropping his shotgun and reaching for his head.

Don Harris turned at the sound just to see the shadow of a man ducking into a door off the hallway. It was all the chance the other guys needed, and Brian hit Harris in the left arm with a throwing star, causing him to drop his own shotgun. The next thing Harris knew he was on the ground with a knee in his back and a thick arm around his neck. The throwing star was still buried an inch deep in his bicep.

Terry emerged from the office with his Beretta in hand and approached the group. Lance let up the pressure on Harris's neck and dragged him up into a seated position. Brian had the shotguns propped against a wall far from the others. Marcel had Dodd covered.

"I told you fuckos you picked the wrong fucking place," Lance said to Dodd.

• • •

Sheriff Baker had been concerned when he talked to Decker, but now he was legitimately worried. He'd paged Terry an hour ago and gotten no response. After a few minutes he tried calling the Beam Reach, thinking maybe he was working and didn't notice the page. But Wendy told him he'd left more than an hour ago. So he paged Terry again. Still no answer.

He decided he couldn't wait around at home, and got in his patrol car headed for the marina. He hoped Terry was just hanging out on *Easy Goer* and didn't have the pager on him. But he'd never really seen Terry without the pager on him.

• • •

The guys at the dojo had phoned for an ambulance for Jeremey Dodd, who almost certainly was suffering from a concussion. While they were waiting, they asked Don Harris a few questions about what he and his friend were doing there. Harris didn't feel like talking. He made a bunch of threats instead.

Terry went back to the office to call the sheriff. Before he picked up the phone, he remembered his pager in the desk drawer. He saw three calls from the sheriff's home number. The sheriff wasn't one to call three times in the span of an hour, so he was immediately on alert. He decided to call back.

"Hey, Cindy, it's Terry. Is Tim there?"

"Oh, no. He went over to the marina looking for you. Is everything all right, Terry?" she asked.

"It's kinda complicated. I've gotta reach Tim."

He hung up and called the sheriff's department.

"I need you to patch me through to Sheriff Baker's car. It's an emergency."

"Sir, if this is an emergency, you need to dial 911, and an officer will ..."

"This is not that kind of emergency. I need the sheriff personally. I'm a reserve deputy with the department." He read off his badge number.

Finally he got through.

"Sheriff," he said into the phone.

"Terry!" the sheriff said. "Where the hell are you?"

"I'm at the dojo. Look, Tim, a couple of assholes busted in here with shotguns and ski masks threatening the guys. Everyone's OK, and we've got it under control, but ..."

"Shit, Terry," the sheriff said, cutting him off. "I got a call from Decker tonight at home. Somebody was checking out your records at the DMV, and Decker thinks it's someone involved with the murders up there."

"Ah, fuck," Terry said. Then it hit him: His DMV records would show his address as the house he'd once shared with his wife. "Mallory!"

"Yeah, she might be in danger. I'm heading over there."

"I am too. One more thing."

"What's that?"

"Can you send a car to pick up the douchebag we caught here?"

"I thought you said there were two douchebags."

"We've got an ambulance coming for the other one."

"Roger that," the sheriff said.

After hanging up with the sheriff, Terry had another thought: *I need to tell Vin. His son could be just as much of a target as I am.*

Terry ran out of the office and hurriedly said to Lance: "I gotta go. Someone needs to call this number," pulling up Vin Capriani's phone number in his pager's memory. "It's Vin Capriani. Tell him that you're a friend of Terry Cahill, that his son might be in danger, and he needs to get some guys to the hospital." He tossed the pager to Brian.

"What's going on?" Lance asked. "Where are you going?"

"They may be after me," Terry said. "Sheriff said they might be heading to my old house. My ex-wife ..."

"I'm going with you," Lance said.

"Then come on."

"You guys stay here with those shitbirds," Lance said to Brian and Marcel.

"Yeah, like you need to tell us," Marcel said. He was holding a Katana and grinning.

Lance ducked into the office and reemerged holding a stainless steel Colt Government Model Series 80. He racked a round into the chamber and thumbed the safety on, stuffing the gun in his waistband as he ran to Terry's Buick.

Terry fired up the engine and floored the accelerator, sliding the big car around in a lurid U-turn on Front Street, both rear tires smoking all the way. He hooked a left on South Kalorama Street and cut over to Main, pushing the car up to 70 mph on Main, the big-block engine roaring. He got to the corner of McKinley and Virginia just in time to see the sheriff pulling up on Virginia Street.

They all got out of their cars. Terry and Lance were approaching the sheriff's car when Lance stopped, holding Terry back, and pointed.

In the shadows around the house, a man dressed in dark clothing was approaching a window of Terry's house on the McKinley Street side. He was holding something. They heard the distinct click of a Zippo lighter opening, and in the flame it created they could see what looked like a bottle with a rag hanging out of the mouth.

The man never got a chance to light the molotov cocktail he was planning to throw through Terry's former bedroom window. There was the sound of a muffled pop, and the man fell. The sheriff, Terry, and Lance all turned toward the source of the sound. They saw a black Lexus LS400 pull from the curb on McKinley and accelerate sharply away, its lights still turned off.

The three men ran to the lawn where the man fell. The lighter was still flickering in his hand. The bullet had made a mess of Deputy Kirkham's chest, entering between the shoulder blades and leaving a bloody, fist-sized hole on the other side. He gasped a few times before losing consciousness. There was no point in checking for a pulse. His heart had clearly been shredded by the projectile.

Mallory Cahill came out the front door of her house and saw Terry there with Lance and the sheriff.

"Terry, what's going on?" she asked.

"Please go back inside, Mal," Terry said. "It might not be safe out here."

"What's going on?" she repeated.

"Go in with her," the sheriff said. "Keep her inside, and call an ambulance for this guy." He looked over at Lance. "You go in with them. Keep that gun in easy reach. I'm going to search the perimeter, get some cars out here."

Terry walked over to his soon-to-be ex-wife and said: "Let's go in."

"Is that a gun?" she asked as they were walking to the door.

37

Aftermath

Kerry Kirkham died on Mallory Cahill's lawn. He didn't have much of a chance. The bullet that passed through him was found in the siding of the house. It had been a .45 caliber hollow-point, the kind cops used to call "flying ashtrays."

Nobody had gotten the license plate of the Lexus that drove away after the shot. For what it was worth, nobody really knew for sure whether the shot had even come from the Lexus, but none of the men who were there when it happened would bet against it.

The murder of Deputy Kirkham was unsolved for the time. The only leads were the bullet and the car. There were hundreds, maybe thousands of black LS400s in Southern California. They didn't have much hope of a ballistics match on the bullet, either. Forty-five caliber was pretty popular too among gun owners, and any gunman with two functioning brain cells knew to ditch a weapon right after using it. There was a big ocean right next door, and the .45 was probably somewhere on the bottom of it.

But while Kirkham's murder was still an open case with a dismal prognosis, the murders of Bradley Keener and Danielle Winfield were not. Kirkham's car, a '73 Chevy Nova coupe, was found parked half a block away from the Cahill house. Sheriff's deputies searching the car found a set of keys underneath the driver's seat. Working with Detective Decker of the Santa Barbara's Sheriff's Department and Master Chief Donnelly of the U.S. Coast Guard, they quickly determined the keys belonged to Keener.

A search of Kirkham's home found a set of weights with markings consistent with the impressions left in the carpet in the back of Keener's Ramcharger. The two 10-kg. weights were missing from the set. It wasn't as good as a set of fingerprints, but it was enough for Detective Decker.

He reviewed the security footage from the hospital on the night Jonathan Abernathy was killed, and while he couldn't make a positive ID, the man in the latex gloves fit Kirkham's general description. It wouldn't be enough to convict the man in court, but then, Kirkham didn't live to see a courthouse anyway.

With what he suspected regarding Abernathy's drug-fueled sexual assaults, Decker braced Billy Newhouse. Under pressure, Newhouse cracked. He admitted knowledge of Jon-Jon's activities, but denied participation in them. Decker didn't believe him and threatened him with a lengthy stay in a correctional facility. And then he brought up Danielle Winfield.

Newhouse spilled all. He had been on the beach when Jon-Jon murdered Winfield. He and the other men present conspired with Deputy Kirkham to cover up the death as an accident. In exchange for a reduced sentence, he gave up the rest of the Santa Barbara Boys who'd been involved, including Dewey Michaels.

Michaels would later claim that Newhouse had extorted him after the fact. He needed the money to buy his share of Shockley's Tavern.

Jeremey Dodd recovered from the concussion he received courtesy of Cahill's thrown beer bottle. He was fortunate to not have a fractured skull. Both he and Don Harris decided to testify against the other Santa Barbara Boys for their roles in intimidating and assaulting beachgoers at Rincon Point. Both men denied any knowledge of Deputy Kirkham's intent to firebomb the Cahill house in Ventura.

Harris also agreed to provide testimony in the event that Jon-Jon's sexual assaults should ever become a point of evidence in any trial. Dodd claimed memory loss, which Decker didn't believe for a second, but he knew a court would consider it reasonable doubt.

All told, it turned out fairly well for Rick Decker. He was only getting credit for solving the murders of Brad Keener and Danielle Winfield, but that still looked good. Besides, Decker knew he was near the end of a long and well-regarded career, having joined the S.B.S.D. only after retiring from L.A.P.D. Robbery-Homicide five years ago. He didn't need to prove himself to anyone.

He was sure that Abernathy and Scott Keener had been killed by Deputy Kirkham as well, but the department wasn't terribly keen to double the number of kills connected to one of their own. Decker would have to live with that, and decided that with both of the killers in the ground he probably could. As for Kirkham's murder, well, that was Sheriff Baker's problem, wasn't it?

38

Housewarming

It was now a week after the events that night on the corner of McKinley and Virginia. Terry Cahill was feeling pretty good, even though seeing a man dying on what was once his lawn had shaken him. But today was a new day.

He was having friends over to his new place, an apartment he was renting on South Laurel Street. It was an older building, but well maintained and neatly kept. There was a wall-unit air conditioner in the bedroom. He'd bought mostly cheap, second-hand furniture for the place, except for the bed, which he bought new. He didn't like the idea of sleeping on a used mattress. Terry made a batch of his chili for his guests, who were starting to arrive.

The first one over was Wendy. She'd seen him make the chili enough times to know how to make it herself now, but that was all right with Terry. It meant he didn't always have to make the huge batches the bar was selling all by himself anymore.

"Thanks for giving Charlie a home," she said, nodding toward the gray and white cat, who had hopped on a kitchen counter to investigate.

"I think we may have bonded. Anyway, I couldn't just leave him there. I like having him around." Charlie seemed to approve of his new digs. He walked over to Wendy for a head scratch.

Wendy had brought some booze over and was mixing up a batch of margaritas when the other guests arrived.

Lance, Brian, Marcel, Arturo and Sheriff Baker all came in, each carrying a six-pack of the kind of cheap beer Terry loved.

"Aw, you shouldn't have, guys," Terry said. He was happy to see all of them.

"Hey, this place isn't bad," Sheriff Baker said.

"What, you expected me to live in some kind of dump?" Terry asked playfully.

"I did, judging by that car you drive," Lance chimed in.

"I guess I should give this back," Terry said, handing his badge over to Tim.

"Hold onto it for a while," Tim said. "At least until you get your P.I. license."

"P.I. license?"

"You're a good investigator, Terry. You've got a talent for it. You said yourself you're not going back into journalism. I think you should get your license and keep doing what you're good at. I can grease the wheels for you with the state. In the meantime, I'll put you through a couple of courses at the academy so you can remain a reserve deputy."

"I don't know what to say."

"A simple yes will suffice."

Even Vin Capriani stopped by. Terry hadn't invited him, but he wasn't about to be rude to the man. He brought with him a copy of the *Ventura Voyager*, a free weekly newspaper that one of his companies published. It had the story Cahill had written up regarding the case. Terry guessed that Vin had been fucking with him on that first meeting, when he'd said he planned to publish the story in a pornographic magazine.

"Thought you'd like to see your name in print again," Vin said, handing him the tabloid. "You did good work, kid. I owe you one."

"Thanks, Vin, but you already paid me."

"Some debts cannot be paid with money alone. That call you had your guy make to me? About sending someone off to protect my son? It means a lot to me that you would think of that when you had your own shit to worry about. I will always consider you a friend for that."

"You're welcome."

"Well, I gotta run. I just wanted to stop by, give you a copy of the paper. You ever have more stories, give me a call."

Terry watched Vin Capriani walk down to the curb, where he reached for the passenger door handle of a large black Lexus sedan.

"Hey, Vin," Terry called out.

Vin turned before getting into the passenger seat.

"Yeah, kid?"

"Nice car."

Vin winked at him.

Author's Note

This book makes reference to sharks attacking people on California beaches. I want to point out that shark attacks are exceptionally rare, not just here, but anywhere. Sharks are not mindless killing machines out to make a quick meal out of anyone who wanders into the ocean. Recent discoveries have found that sharks are far more common in the waters off California's coast than previously had been believed, and that many swimmers, surfers, paddle boarders, kayakers, etcetera have encountered sharks without even knowing it. They didn't know because the sharks peacefully swam by, unnoticed.

Yet several thousand sharks are killed each year. By us. Whether accidentally caught in commercial fishing operations, or deliberately caught for purposes such as making shark fin soup, we kill a *lot* more sharks than they us. Shark fin soup is a particularly cruel dish, as the sharks have their fins cut off and are thrown back into the water to die a slow death. Please make no mistake about it: The most dangerous creature on the water is us.

Made in the USA
Columbia, SC
24 September 2022